CAPE COD STORIES

OR

THE "OLD HOME HOUSE"

"SHE JIBED—OH, YES—SHE JIBED!"

Cape Cod Stories

FORMERLY PUBLISHED UNDER THE TITLE OF
"THE OLD HOME HOUSE"

By JOSEPH C. LINCOLN

Author of "Mr. Pratt," "Cap'n Eri," "Partners of the
Tide," "The Depot Master," etc.

WITH ILLUSTRATIONS

Fredonia Books
Amsterdam, The Netherlands

Cape Cod Stories

by Joseph C. Lincoln

ISBN 1-58963-000-9

Copyright © 2001 by Fredonia Books

Reprinted from the 1907 edition

Fredonia Books
Amsterdam, The Netherlands
http://www.FredoniaBooks.com

In order to make original editions of historical works available to scholars at an economical price, this facsimile of the original edition of 1907 is reproduced from the best available copy and has been digitally enhanced to improve legibility, but the text remains unaltered to retain historical authenticity.

CONTENTS

▼

CONTENTS

ILLUSTRATIONS

THE "OLD HOME HOUSE"

TWO PAIRS OF SHOES

I don't exactly know why Cap'n Jonadab and me went to the post-office that night; we wa'n't expecting any mail, that's sartin. I guess likely we done it for the reason the feller that tumbled overboard went to the bottom—'twas the handiest place *to* go.

Anyway we was there, and I was propping up the stove with my feet and holding down a chair with the rest of me, when Jonadab heaves alongside flying distress signals. He had an envelope in his starboard mitten, and, coming to anchor with a flop in the next chair, sets shifting the thing from one hand to the other as if it 'twas red hot.

I watched this performance for a spell, waiting for him to say something, but he didn't, so I hailed, kind of sarcastic, and says: "What you doing—playing solitaire? Which hand's ahead?"

He kind of woke up then, and passes the envelope over to me.

"Barzilla," he says, "what in time do you s'pose that is?"

'Twas a queer looking envelope, more'n the average length fore and aft, but kind of scant in the beam. There was a puddle of red sealing wax on the back of it with a "D" in the middle, and up in one corner was a kind of picture thing in colors, with some printing in a foreign language underneath it. I b'lieve 'twas what they call a "coat-of-arms," but it looked more like a patchwork comforter than it did like any coat ever I see. The envelope was addressed to "Captain Jonadab Wixon, Orham, Mass."

I took my turn at twisting the thing around, and then I hands it back to Jonadab.

"I pass," I says. "Where'd you get it?"

"'Twas in my box," says he. "Must have come in to-night's mail."

I didn't know the mail was sorted, but when he says that I got up and went over and unlocked my box, just to show that I hadn't forgot how, and I swan to man if there wa'n't another envelope, just like Jonadab's, except that 'twas addressed to "Barzilla Wingate."

"Humph!" says I, coming back to the stove;

"you ain't the only one that's heard from the Prince of Wales. Look here!"

He was the most surprised man, but one, on the Cape: I was the one. We couldn't make head nor tail of the business, and set there comparing the envelopes, and wondering who on earth had sent 'em. Pretty soon "Ily" Tucker heads over towards our moorings, and says he: "What's troubling the ancient mariners?" he says.

"Barzilla and me's got a couple of letters," says Cap'n Jonadab; "and we was wondering who they was from."

Tucker leaned away down—he's always suffering from a rush of funniness to the face—and he whispers, awful solemn: "For heaven's sake, whatever you do, don't open 'em. You might find out." Then he threw off his main-hatch and "haw-hawed" like a loon.

To tell you the truth, we hadn't thought of opening 'em—not yet—so that was kind of one on us, as you might say. But Jonadab ain't so slow but he can catch up with a hearse if the horses stop to drink, and he comes back quick.

"Ily," he says, looking troubled, "you ought to sew reef-points on your mouth. 'Tain't safe to open the whole of it on a windy night like this. First thing you know you'll carry away the top of your head."

Well, we felt consider'ble better after that—
having held our own on the tack, so to speak—
and we walked out of the post-office and up to
my room in the Travellers' Rest, where we could
be alone. Then we opened up the envelopes,
both at the same time. Inside of each of 'em
was another envelope, slick and smooth as a
mack'rel's back, and inside of *that* was a letter,
printed, but looking like the kind of writing that
used to be in the copybook at school. It said
that Ebenezer Dillaway begged the honor of our
presence at the marriage of his daughter, Belle,
to Peter Theodosius Brown, at Dillamead House,
Cashmere-on-the-Hudson, February three, nine-
teen hundred and so forth.

We were surprised, of course, and pleased in
one way, but in another we wa'n't real tickled to
death. You see, 'twas a good while sence Jona-
bad and me had been to a wedding, and we know
there'd be mostly young folks there and a good
many big-bugs, we presumed likely, and 'twas
going to cost consider'ble to get rigged—not to
mention the price of passage, and one thing a'
'nother. But Ebenezer had took the trouble to
write us, and so we felt 'twas our duty not to
disappoint him, and especially Peter, who had
done so much for us, managing the Old Home
House.

The Old Home House was our summer hotel at Wellmouth Port. How me and Jonadab come to be in the summer boarding trade is another story and it's too long to tell now. We never would have been in it, anyway, I cal'late, if it hadn't been for Peter. He made a howling success of our first season and likewise helped himself along by getting engaged to the star boarder, rich old Dillaway's daughter—Ebenezer Dillaway, of the Consolidated Cash Stores.

Well, we see 'twas our duty to go, so we went. I had a new Sunday cutaway and light pants to go with it, so I figgered that I was pretty well found, but Cap'n Jonadab had to pry himself loose from considerable money, and every cent hurt as if 'twas nailed on. Then he had chilblains that winter, and all the way over in the Fall River boat he was fuming about them chilblains, and adding up on a piece of paper how much cash he'd spent.

We struck Cashmere-on-the-Hudson about three o'clock on the afternoon of the day of the wedding. 'Twas a little country kind of a town, smaller by a good deal than Orham, and so we cal'lated that perhaps after all, the affair wouldn't be so everlasting tony. But when we hove in sight of Dillamead—Ebenezer's place—we shortened sail and pretty nigh drew out of the race.

'Twas up on a high bank over the river, and the house itself was bigger than four Old Homes spliced together. It had a fair-sized township around it in the shape of land, with a high stone wall for trimming on the edges. There was trees, and places for flower-beds in summer, and the land knows what. We see right off that this was the real Cashmere-on-the-Hudson; the village folks were stranded on the flats—old Dillaway filled the whole ship channel.

"Well," I says to Jonadab, "it looks to me as if we was getting out of soundings. What do you say to coming about and making a quick run for Orham again?"

But he wouldn't hear of it. "S'pose I've spent all that money on duds for nothing?" he says. "No, sir, by thunder! I ain't scared of Peter Brown, nor her that's going to be his wife; and I ain't scared of Ebenezer neither; no matter if he does live in the Manufacturers' Building, with two or three thousand fathom of front fence," he says.

Some years ago Jonadab got reckless and went on a cut-rate excursion to the World's Fair out in Chicago, and ever sence then he's been comparing things with the "Manufacturers' Building" or the "Palace of Agriculture" or "Streets of Cairo," or some other outlandish place.

"All right," says I. "Darn the torpedoes! Keep her as she is! You can fire when ready, Gridley!"

So we sot sail for what we jedged was Ebenezer's

We Hove in Sight of Dillamead.

front-gate, and just as we made it, a man comes whistling round the bend in the path, and I'm blessed if 'twa'n't Peter T. Brown. He was rigged to kill, as usual, only more so.

"Hello, Peter!" I says. "Here we be."

If ever a feller was surprised, Brown was that feller. He looked like he'd struck a rock where there was deep water on the chart.

"Well, I'll be ——" he begun, and then stopped. "What in the ——" he commenced again, and again his breath died out. Fin'lly he says: "Is this you, or had I better quit and try another pipe?"

We told him 'twas us, and it seemed to me that he wa'n't nigh so tickled as he'd ought to have been. When he found we'd come to the wedding, 'count of Ebenezer sending us word, he didn't say nothing for a minute or so.

"Of course, we *had* to come," says Jonadab. "We felt 'twouldn't be right to disapp'int Mr. Dillaway."

Peter kind of twisted his mouth. "That's so," he says. "It'll be worth more'n a box of diamonds to him. Do him more good than joining a 'don't worry club.' Well, come on up to the house and ease his mind."

So we done it, and Ebenezer acted even more surprised than Peter.

I can't tell you anything about that house, nor the fixings in it; it beat me a mile—that house did. We had a room somewheres up on the hurricane deck, with brass bunks and plush carpets and crocheted curtains and electric lights. I swan there was looking glasses in every corner—

big ones, man's size. I remember Cap'n Jonadab hollering to me that night when he was getting ready to turn in:

"For the land's sake, Barzilla!" says he, "turn out them lights, will you? I ain't over'n' above bashful, but them looking glasses make me feel's if I was undressing along with all hands and the cook."

The house was full of comp'ny, and more kept coming all the time. Swells! don't talk! We felt 'bout as much at home as a cow in a dory, but we was there 'cause Ebenezer had asked us to be there, so we kept on the course and didn't signal for help. Travelling through the rooms down stairs where the folks was, was a good deal like dodging icebergs up on the Banks, but one or two noticed us enough to dip the colors, and one was real sociable. He was a kind of slow-spoken city-feller, dressed as if his clothes was poured over him hot and then left to cool. His last name had a splice in the middle of it— 'twas Catesby-Stuart. Everybody—that is, most everybody—called him "Phil."

Well, sir, Phil cottoned to Jonadab and me right away. He'd get us, one on each wing, and go through that house asking questions. He pumped me and Jonadab dry about how we come to be there, and told us more yarns than a few 'bout Dillaway, and how rich he was. I remember he said that he only wished he had the keys to the cellar so he could show us the money-bins. Said Ebenezer was so just—well, rotten with money, as you might say, that he kept it in bins down cellar, same as poor folks kept coal —gold in one bin, silver half-dollars in another, quarters in another, and so on. When he needed any, he'd say to a servant: "James, fetch me up a hod of change." This was only one of the fish yarns he told. They sounded kind of scaly to Jonadab and me, but if we hinted at such a thing, he'd pull himself together and say: "Fact, I assure you," in a way to freeze your vitals. He seemed like such a good feller that we didn't mind his telling a few big ones; we'd known good fellers afore that liked to lie—gunners and such like, they were mostly.

Somehow or 'nother Phil got Cap'n Jonadab talking "boat," and when Jonadab talks "boat" there ain't no stopping him. He's the smartest feller in a cat-boat that ever handled a tiller, and he's won more races than any man on the Cape, I cal'late. Phil asked him and me if we'd ever sailed on an ice-boat, and, when we said we hadn't he asks if we won't take a sail with him on the river next morning. We didn't want to put him to so much trouble on our account, but he said: "Not at all. Pleasure'll be all mine, I assure you." Well, 'twas his for a spell—but never mind that now.

He introduced us to quite a lot of the comp'ny —men mostly. He'd see a school of 'em in a corner, or under a palm tree or somewheres, and steer us over in that direction and make us known to all hands. Then he begin to show us off, so to speak, get Jonadab telling 'bout the boats he'd sailed, or something like it—and them fellers would laugh and holler, but Phil's face wouldn't shake out a reef: he looked solemn as a fun'ral all the time. Jonadab and me begun to think we was making a great hit. Well, we was, but not the way we thought. I remember one of the gang gets Phil to one side after a talk like this and whispers to him, laughing like fun. Phil says to him: "My dear boy, I've been to thousands of these things——" waving his flipper scornful around the premises—"and upon honor they've all been alike. Now that I've discovered something positively original, let me enjoy myself. The entertainment by the Heavenly Twins is only begun."

I didn't know what he meant then; I do now.

The marrying was done about eight o'clock and done with all the trimmings. All hands manned the yards in the best parlor, and Peter and Belle was hitched. Then they went away in a swell turnout—not like the derelict hacks we'd seen stranded by the Cashmere depot—and Jonadab pretty nigh took the driver's larboard ear off with a shoe Phil gave him to heave after 'em.

After the wedding the folks was sitting under the palms and bushes that was growing in tubs all over the house, and the stewards—there was enough of 'em to man a four-master—was carting 'round punch and frozen victuals. Everybody was togged up till Jonadab and me, in our new cutaways, felt like a couple of moulting black-birds at a blue-jay camp-meeting. Ebenezer was so busy, flying 'round like a pullet with its head off, that he'd hardly spoke to us sence we landed, but Phil scarcely ever left us, so we wa'n't lonesome. Pretty soon he comes back from a beat into the next room, and he says:

"There's a lady here that's just dying to know you gentlemen. Her name's Granby. Tell her all about the Cape; she'll like it. And, by the way, my dear feller," he whispers to Jonadab "if you want to please her—er—mightily, con-gratulate her upon her boy's success in the laundry business. You understand," he says, winking; "only son and self-made man, don't you know."

Mrs. Granby was roosting all by herself on a sofy in the parlor. She was fleshy, but terrible stiff and proud, and when she moved the diamonds on her shook till her head and neck looked like one of them "set pieces" at the Fourth of July fireworks. She was deef, too, and used an ear-trumpet pretty nigh as big as a steamer's ventilator.

Maybe she was "dying to know us," but she didn't have a fit trying to show it. Me and Jonadab felt we'd ought to be sociable, and so we set, one on each side of her on the sofy, and bellered: "How d'ye do?" and "Fine day, ain't it?" into that ear-trumpet. She didn't say much, but she'd couple on the trumpet and turn to whichever one of us had hailed, heeling over to that side as if her ballast had shifted. She acted to me kind of uneasy, but everybody that come into that parlor—and they kept piling in all the time—looked more'n middling joyful. They kept pretty quiet, too, so that every yell we let out echoed, as you might say, all 'round. I begun to git shaky at the knees, as if I was preaching to a big congregation.

After a spell, Jonadab not being able to think of anything more to say, and remembering Phil's orders, leans over and whoops into the trumpet.

"I'm real glad your son done so well with his laundry," he says.

Well, sir, Phil had give us to understand that them congratulations would make a hit, and they done it. The women 'round the room turned red and some of 'em covered their mouths with their handkerchiefs. The men looked glad and set up and took notice. Ebenezer wa'n't in the room—which was a mercy—but your old messmate, Catesby-Stuart, looked solemn as ever and never turned a hair.

But as for old lady Granby—whew! She got redder'n she was afore, which was a miracle, pretty nigh. She couldn't speak for a minute—just cackled like a hen. Then she busts out with: "How dare you!" and flounces out of that room like a hurricane. And it was still as could be for a minute, and then two or three of the girls begun to squeal and giggle behind their handkerchiefs.

Jonadab and me went away, too. We didn't flounce any to speak of. I guess a "sneak" would come nearer to telling how we quit. I see the cap'n heading for the stairs and I fell into his wake. Nobody said good-night, and we didn't wait to give 'em a chance.

'Course we knew we'd put our foot in it somewheres, but we didn't see just how. Even then we wa'n't really onto Phil's game. You see, when a green city chap comes to the Old Home House—and the land knows there's freaks enough do come—we always try to make things pleasant for him, and the last thing we'd think of was making him a show afore folks. So we couldn't b'lieve even now 'twas done a-purpose. But we was suspicious, a little.

"Barzilla," says Jonadab, getting ready to turn in, "'tain't possible that that feller with the sprained last name is having fun with us, is it?"

"Jonadab," says I, "I've been wondering that myself."

And we wondered for an hour, and finally decided to wait a while and say nothing till we could ask Ebenezer. And the next morning one of the stewards comes up to our room with some coffee and grub, and says that Mr. Catesby-Stuart requested the pleasure of our comp'ny on a afore-breakfast ice-boat sail, and would meet us at the pier in half an hour. They didn't have breakfast at Ebenezer's till pretty close to dinner time, eleven o'clock, so we had time enough for quite a trip.

Phil and the ice-boat met us on time. I s'pose it 'twas style, but, if I hadn't known I'd have swore he'd run short of duds and had dressed up in the bed-clothes. I felt of his coat when he wa'n't noticing, and if it wa'n't made out of a blanket then I never slept under one. And it made me think of my granddad to see what he had on his head—a reg'lar nightcap, tassel and all.

Phil said he was sorry we turned in so early the night afore. Said he'd planned to entertain us all the evening. We didn't hurrah much at this—being suspicious, as I said—and he changed the subject to ice-boats.

That ice-boat was a bird. I cal'lated to know a boat when I sighted one, but a flat-iron on skates was something bran-new. I didn't think much of it, and I could see that Jonadab didn't neither.

But in about three shakes of a lamb's tail I was ready to take it all back and say I never said it. I done enough praying in the next half hour to square up for every Friday night meeting I'd missed sence I was a boy. Phil got sail onto her, and we moved out kind of slow.

"Now, then," says he, "we'll take a little jaunt up the river. 'Course this isn't like one of your Cape Cod cats, but still——"

And then I dug my finger nails into the deck and commenced: "Now I lay me." Talk about going! 'Twas "F-s-s-s-t!" and we was a mile from home. "Bu-z-z-z!" and we was just getting ready to climb a bank; but 'fore she nosed the shore Phil would put the helm over and we'd whirl round like a windmill, with me and Jonadab biting the planking, and hanging on for dear life, and my heart, that had been up in my mouth knocking the soles of my boots off. And Cap'n Catesby-Stuart would grin, and drawl: "'Course, this ain't like a Orham cat-boat, but she does fairly well—er—fairly. Now, for instance, how does this strike you?"

It struck us—I don't think any got away. I expected every minute to land in the hereafter, and it got so that the prospect looked kind of inviting, if only to get somewheres where 'twas warm. That February wind went in at the top of my stiff hat and whizzed out through the legs of my thin Sunday pants till I felt for all the world like the ventilating pipe on an ice-chest. I could see why Phil was wearing the bed-clothes; what I was suffering for just then was a feather mattress on each side of me.

Well, me and Jonadab was "it" for quite a spell. Phil had all the fun, and I guess he enjoyed it. If he'd stopped right then, when the fishing was good, I cal'late he'd have fetched port with a full hold; but no, he had to rub it in, so to speak, and that's where he slopped over. You know how 'tis when you're eating mince-pie—it's the "one more slice" that fetches the nightmare. Phil stopped to get that slice.

He kept whizzing up and down that river till Jonadab and me kind of got over our variousness. We could manage to get along without spreading out like porous plasters, and could set up for a minute or so on a stretch. And twa'n't necessary for us to hold a special religious service every time the flat-iron come about. Altogether, we was in that condition where the doctor might have held out some hopes.

And, in spite of the cold, we was noticing how Phil was sailing that three-cornered sneak-box— noticing and criticising; at least, I was, and Cap'n Jonadab, being, as I've said, the best skipper of small craft from Provincetown to Cohasset Narrows, must have had some ideas on the subject. Your old chum, Catesby-Stuart, thought he was mast-high so fur's sailing was concerned, anybody could see that, but he had something to larn. He wasn't beginning to get out all there was in that ice-boat. And just then along comes another feller in the same kind of hooker and gives us a hail. There was two other chaps on the boat with him.

"Hello, Phil!" he yells, rounding his flat-iron into the wind abreast of ours and bobbing his night-cap. "I hoped you might be out. Are you game for a race?"

"Archie," answers our skipper, solemn as a setting hen, "permit me to introduce to you Cap'n Jonadab Wixon and Admiral Barzilla Wingate, of Orham, on the Cape."

I wasn't expecting to fly an admiral's pennant quite so quick, but I managed to shake out through my teeth—they was chattering like a box of dice—that I was glad to know the feller. Jonadab, he rattled loose something similar.

"The Cap'n and the Admiral," says Phil, "having sailed the raging main for lo! these many years, are now favoring me with their advice concerning the navigation of ice-yachts. Archie, if you're willing to enter against such a handicap of brains and barnacles, I'll race you on a beat up to the point yonder, then on the ten mile run afore the wind to the buoy opposite the Club, and back to the cove by Dillaway's. And we'll make it a case of wine. Is it a go?"

Archie, he laughed and said it was, and, all at once, the race was on.

Now, Phil had lied when he said we was "favoring" him with advice, 'cause we hadn't said a word; but that beat up to the point wa'n't half over afore Jonadab and me was dying to tell him a few things. He handled that boat like a lobster. Archie gained on every tack and come about for the run a full minute afore us.

And on that run afore the wind 'twas worse than ever. The way Phil see-sawed that piece of pie back and forth over the river was a sin and shame. He could have slacked off his mainsail and headed dead for the buoy, but no, he jiggled around like an old woman crossing the road ahead of a funeral.

Cap'n Jonadab was on edge. Racing was where he lived, as you might say, and he fidgeted like he was setting on a pin-cushion. By and by he snaps out:

"Keep her off! Keep her off afore the wind! Can't you see where you're going?"

Phil looked at him as if he was a graven image, and all the answer he made was; "Be calm, Barnacles, be calm!"

But pretty soon I couldn't stand it no longer, and I busts out with: "Keep her off, Mr. What's-your name! For the Lord's sake, keep her off! He'll beat the life out of you!"

And all the good that done was for me to get a stare that was colder than the wind, if such a thing's possible.

But Jonadab got fidgetyer every minute, and when we come out into the broadest part of the river, within a little ways of the buoy, he couldn't stand it no longer.

"You're spilling half the wind!" he yells. "Pint' her for the buoy or else you'll be licked to death! Jibe her so's she gits it full. Jibe her, you lubber! Don't you know how? Here! let me show you!"

And the next thing I knew he fetched a hop like a frog, shoved Phil out of the way, grabbed the tiller, and jammed it over.

She jibed—oh, yes, she jibed! If anybody says she didn't you send 'em to me. I give you my word that that flat-iron jibed twice—once for practice, I jedge, and then for business. She commenced by twisting and squirming like an eel. I jest had sense enough to clamp my mittens onto the little brass rail by the stern and hold on; then she jibed the second time. She stood up on two legs, the boom come over with a slat that pretty nigh took the mast with it, and the whole shebang whirled around as if it had forgot something. I have a foggy kind of remembrance of locking my mitten clamps fast onto that rail while the rest of me streamed out in the air like a burgee. Next thing I knew we was scooting back towards Dillaway's, with the sail catching every ounce that was blowing. Jonadab was braced across the tiller, and there, behind us, was the Honorable Philip Catesby-Stuart, flat on his back, with his blanket legs looking like a pair of compasses, and skimming in whirligigs over the slick ice towards Albany. *He* hadn't had nothing to hold onto, you understand. Well, if I hadn't seen it, I wouldn't have b'lieved that a human being could spin so long or travel so fast on his back. His legs made a kind of smoky circle in the air over him, and he'd got such a start I thought he'd *never stop* a-going. He come to a place where some snow had melted in the sun and there was a pond, as you might say, on the ice, and he went through that, heaving spray like one of them circular lawn sprinklers the summer folks have. He'd have been as pretty as a fountain, if we'd had time to stop and look at him.

"For the land sakes, heave to!" I yelled, soon's I could get my breath. "You've spilled the skipper!"

"Skipper be durned!" howls Jonadab, squeezing the tiller and keeping on the course; "We'll come back for him by and by. It's our business to win this race."

And, by ginger! we *did* win it. The way Jonadab coaxed that cocked hat on runners over the ice was pretty—yes, sir, pretty! He nipped her close enough to the wind'ard, and he took advantage of every single chance. He always *could* sail; I'll say that for him. We walked up on Archie like he'd set down to rest, and passed him afore he was within a half mile of home. We run up abreast of Dillaway's, putting on all the fancy frills of a liner coming into port, and there was Ebenezer and a whole crowd of wedding company down by the landing.

"Gosh!" says Jonadab, tugging at his whiskers:
"'Twas Cape Cod against New York that time,
and you can't beat the Cape when it comes to
getting over water, not even if the water's froze.
Hey, Barzilla ? "

Ebenezer came hopping over the ice towards
us. He looked some surprised.

"Where's Phil ? " he says.

Now, I'd clean forgot Phil and I guess Jonadab
had, by the way he colored up.

"Phil ? " says he. "Phil ? Oh, yes! We left
him up the road a piece. Maybe we'd better go
after him now."

But old Dillaway had something to say.

"Cap'n," he says, looking round to make sure
none of the comp'ny was follering him out to the
ice-boat. "I've wanted to speak to you afore,
but I haven't had the chance. You mustn't
b'lieve too much of what Mr. Catesby-Stuart
says, nor you mustn't always do just what he
suggests. You see," he says, "he's a dreadful
practical joker."

"Yes," says Jonadab, beginning to look sick.
I didn't say nothing, but I guess I looked the
same way.

"Yes," said Ebenezer, kind of uneasy like;
"Now, in that matter of Mrs. Granby. I s'pose
Phil put you up to asking her about her son's

laundry. Yes? Well, I thought so. You see, the fact is, her boy is a broker down in Wall Street, and he's been caught making some of what they call 'wash sales' of stock. It's against the rules of the Exchange to do that, and the papers have been full of the row. You can see," says Dillaway, "how the laundry question kind of stirred the old lady up. But, Lord! it must have been funny," and he commenced to grin.

I looked at Jonadab, and he looked at me. I thought of Marm Granby, and her being "dying to know us," and I thought of the lies about the "hod of change" and all the rest, and I give you my word *I* didn't grin, not enough to show my wisdom teeth, anyhow. A crack in the ice an inch wide would have held me, with room to spare; I know that.

"Hum!" grunts Jonadab, kind of dry and bitter, as if he'd been taking wormwood tea; "*I* see. He's been having a good time making durn fools out of us."

"Well," says Ebenezer, "not exactly that, p'raps, but——"

And then along comes Archie and his crowd in the other ice-boat.

"Hi!" he yells. "Who sailed that boat of yours? He knew his business all right. I never saw anything better. Phil—why, where *is* Phil?"

I answered him. "Phil got out when we jibed," I says.

"Was *that* Phil?" he hollers, and then the three of 'em just roared.

"Oh, by Jove, you know!" says Archie, "that's the funniest thing I ever saw. And on Phil, too! He'll never hear the last of it at the club—hey, boys?" And then they just bellered and laughed again.

When they'd gone, Jonadab turned to Ebenezer and he says: "That taking us out on this boat was another case of having fun with the country-men. Hey?"

"I guess so," says Dillaway. "I b'lieve he told one of the guests that he was going to put Cape Cod on ice this morning."

I looked away up the river where a little black speck was just getting to shore. And I thought of how chilly the wind was out there, and how that ice-water must have felt, and what a long ways 'twas from home. And then I smiled, slow and wide; there was a barge load of joy in every half inch of that smile.

"It's a cold day when Phil loses a chance for a joke," says Ebenezer.

"'Tain't exactly what you'd call summery just now," I says. And we hauled down sail, run the ice-boat up to the wharf, and went up to our room to pack our extension cases for the next train.

"You see," says Jonadab, putting in his other shirt, "it's easy enough to get the best of Cape folks on wash sales and lying, but when it comes to boats that's a different pair of shoes."

"I guess Phil'll agree with you," I says.

THE COUNT AND THE MANAGER

THE COUNT AND THE MANAGER

The way we got into the hotel business in the first place come around like this: Me and Cap'n Jonadab went down to Wellmouth Port one day 'long in March to look at some property he'd had left him. Jonadab's Aunt Sophrony had moved kind of sudden from that village to Beulah Land—they're a good ways apart, too—and Cap'n Jonadab had come in for the old farm, he being the only near relative.

When you go to Wellmouth Port you get off the cars at Wellmouth Center and then take Labe Bearse's barge and ride four miles; and then, if the horse don't take a notion to lay down in the road and go to sleep, or a wheel don't come off or some other surprise party ain't sprung on you, you come to a place where there's a Baptist chapel that needs painting, and a little two-for-a-cent store that needs trade, and two or three houses that need building over, and any Lord's quantity of scrub pines and beach grass and sand. Then you take Labe's word for it that you've got to Wellmouth Port and get out of the barge and try to remember you're a church member.

Well, Aunt Sophrony's house was a mile or more from the place where the barge stopped, and Jonadab and me, we hoofed it up there. We bought some cheese and crackers and canned things at the store, 'cause we expected to stay overnight in the house, and knew there wasn't no other way of getting provender.

We got there after a spell and set down on the big piazza with our souls full of gratitude and our boots full of sand. Great, big, old-fashioned house with fourteen big bedrooms in it, big barn, sheds, and one thing or 'nother, and perched right on top of a hill with five or six acres of ground 'round it. And how the March wind did whoop in off the sea and howl and screech lonesomeness through the pine trees! You take it in the middle of the night, with the shutters rattling and the old joists a-creaking and Jonadab snoring like a chap sawing hollow logs, and if it wan't joy then my name ain't Barzilla Wingate. I don't wonder Aunt Sophrony died. I'd have died 'long afore she did if I knew I was checked plumb through to perdition. There'd be some company where I was going, anyhow.

The next morning after ballasting up with the

THE COUNT AND THE MANAGER 31

truck we'd bought at the store—the feller 'most
keeled over when he found we was going to pay
cash for it—we went out on the piazza again,
and looked at the breakers and the pine trees
and the sand, and held our hats on with both
hands.

"Jonadab," says I, "what'll you take for your
heirloom?"

"Well," he says, "Barzilla, the way I feel now,
I think I'd take a return ticket to Orham and be
afraid of being took up for swindling at that."

Neither of us says nothing more for a spell,
and, first thing you know, we heard a carriage
rattling somewhere up the road. I was ship-
wrecked once and spent two days in a boat looking for a sail. When I heard that rattling I felt
just the way I done when I sighted the ship that
picked us up.

"Judas!" says Jonadab, "there's somebody
coming!"

We jumped out of our chairs and put for the
corner of the house. There *was* somebody coming—a feller in a buggy, and he hitched his horse
to the front fence and come whistling up the
walk.

He was a tall chap, with a smooth face, kind
of sharp and knowing, and with a stiff hat set
just a little on one side. His clothes was new

and about a week ahead of up-to-date, his shoes shined till they lit up the lower half of his legs, and his pants was creased so's you could mow with 'em. Cool and slick! Say! in the middle of that deadliness and compared to Jonadab and me, he looked like a bird of Paradise in a coop of moulting pullets.

"Cap'n Wixon?" he says to me, sticking out a gloved flipper.

"Not guilty," says I. "There's the skipper. My name's Wingate."

"Glad to have the pleasure, Mr. Wingate," he says. "Cap'n Wixon, yours truly."

We shook hands, and he took each of us by the arm and piloted us back to the piazza, like a tug with a couple of coal barges. He pulled up a chair, crossed his legs on the rail, reached into the for'ard hatch of his coat and brought out a cigar case.

"Smoke up," he says. We done it—I holding my hat to shut off the wind, while Jonadab used up two cards of matches getting the first light. When we got the cigars to going finally, the feller says:

"My name's Brown—Peter T. Brown. I read about your falling heir to this estate, Cap'n Wixon, in a New Bedford paper. I happened to be in New Bedford then, representing the John B.

Wilkins Unparalleled All Star Uncle Tom's Cabin and Ten Nights in a Bar-room Company. It isn't my reg'lar line, the show bus'ness, but it produced the necessary 'ham and' every day and the excelsior sleep inviter every night, so— but never mind that. Soon as I read the paper I came right down to look at the property. Having rubbered, back I go to Orham to see you. Your handsome and talented daughter says you are over here. That'll be about all—here I am. Now, then, listen to this."

He went under his hatches again, rousted out a sheet of paper, unfolded it and read something like this—I know it by heart:

"The great sea leaps and splashes before you as it leaped and splashed in the old boyhood days. The sea wind sings to you as it sang of old. The old dreams come back to you, the dreams you dreamed as you slumbered upon the cornhusk mattress in the clean, sweet little chamber of the old home. Forgotten are the cares of business, the scramble for money, the ruthless hunt for fame. Here are perfect rest and perfect peace."

"Now what place would you say I was describing?" says the feller.

"Heaven," says Jonadab, looking up, reverent like.

You never see a body more disgusted than Brown.

"Get out!" he snaps. "Do I look like the advance agent of Glory? Listen to this one."

He unfurls another sheet of paper, and goes off on a tack about like this:

"The old home! You who sit in your luxurious apartments, attended by your liveried servants, eating the costly dishes that bring you dyspepsia and kindred evils, what would you give to go back once more to the simple, cleanly living of the old house in the country? The old home, where the nights were cool and refreshing, the sleep deep and sound; where the huckleberry pies that mother fashioned were swimming in fragrant juice, where the shells of the clams for the chowder were snow white and the chowder itself a triumph; where there were no voices but those of the wind and sea; no——"

"Don't!" busts out Jonadab. "Don't! I can't stand it!"

He was mopping his eyes with his red bandanner. I was consider'ble shook up myself. The dear land knows we was more used to huckleberry pies and clam chowder than we was to liveried servants and costly dishes, but there was something in the way that feller read off that slush that just worked the pump handle. A hog would have cried; I know *I* couldn't help it.

As for Peter T. Brown, he fairly crowed.

"It gets you!" he says. "I knew it would. And it'll get a heap of others, too. Well, we can't send 'em back to the old home, but we can trot the old home to them, or a mighty good imitation of it. Here it is; right here!"

And he waves his hand up toward Aunt Sophrony's cast-off palace.

Cap'n Jonadab set up straight and sputtered like a firecracker. A man hates to be fooled.

"Old home!" he snorts. "Old county jail, you mean!"

And then that Brown feller took his feet down off the rail, hitched his chair right in front of Jonadab and me and commenced to talk. And *how* he did talk! Say, he could talk a Hyannis fisherman into a missionary. I wish I could remember all he said; 'twould make a book as big as a dictionary, but 'twould be worth the trouble of writing it down. 'Fore he got through he talked a thousand dollars out of Cap'n Jonadab, and it takes a pretty hefty lecture to squeeze a quarter out of *him*. To make a long yarn short, this was his plan:

He proposed to turn Aunt Sophrony's wind plantation into a hotel for summer boarders.

And it wan't going to be any worn-out, regulation kind of a summer hotel neither.

"Confound it, man!" he says, "they're sick of hot and cold water, elevators, bell wires with a nigger on the end, and all that. There's a raft of old codgers that call themselves 'self-made men'—meanin' that the Creator won't own 'em, and they take the responsibility themselves—that are always wishing they could go somewheres like the shacks where they lived when they were kids. They're always talking about it, and wishing they could go to the old home and rest. Rest! Why, say, there's as much rest to this place as there is sand, and there's enough of that to scour all the knives in creation."

"But 'twill cost so like the dickens to furnish it," I says.

"Furnish it!" says he. "Why, that's just it! It won't cost nothing to furnish it—nothing to speak of. I went through the house day before yesterday—crawled in the kitchen window—oh! it's all right, you can count the spoons—and there's eight of those bedrooms furnished just right, corded bedsteads, painted bureaus with glass knobs, 'God Bless Our Home' and Uncle Jeremiah's coffin plate on the wall, rag mats on the floor, and all the rest. All she needs is a little more of the same stuff, that I can buy 'round here for next to nothing—I used to buy for an auction room—and a little paint and fixings, and there she is. All I want from you folks is a little money—I'll chuck in two hundred and fifty myself—and you two can be proprietors and treasurers if you want to. But active manager and publicity man—that's yours cheerily, Peter Theodosius Brown!" And he slapped his plaid vest.

Well, he talked all the forenoon and all the way to Orham on the train and most of that night. And when he heaved anchor, Jonadab had agreed to put up a thousand and I was in for five hundred and Peter contributed two hundred and fifty and experience and nerve. And the "Old Home House" was off the ways.

And by the first of May 'twas open and ready for business, too. You never see such a driver as that feller Brown was. He had a new wide piazza built all 'round the main buildings, painted everything up fine, hired the three best women cooks in Wellmouth—and there's some good cooks on Cape Cod, too—and a half dozen chamber girls and waiters. He had some trouble getting corded beds and old bureaus for the empty rooms, but he got 'em finally. He bought the last bed of Beriah Burgess, up at East Harniss, and had quite a dicker getting it.

"He thought he ought to get five dollars for

it," says Brown, telling Jonadab and me about it. "Said he hated to part with it because his grandmother died in it. I told him I couldn't see any good reason why I should pay more for a bed just because it had killed his grandmother, so we split up and called it three dollars. 'Twas too much money, but we had to have it."

And the advertisements! They was sent everywheres. Lots of 'em was what Peter called "reading notices," and them he mostly got for nothing, for he could talk an editor foolish same as he could anybody else. By the middle of April most of our money was gone, but every room in the house was let and we had applications coming by the pailful.

And the folks that come had money, too—they had to have to pay Brown's rates. I always felt like a robber or a Standard Oil director every time I looked at the books. The most of 'em was rich folks—self-made men, just like Peter prophesied—and they brought their wives and daughters and slept on cornhusks and eat chowder and said 'twas great and just like old times. And they got the rest we advertised; we didn't cheat 'em on *rest*. By ten o'clock pretty nigh all hands was abed, and 'twas so still all you could hear was the breakers or the wind, or p'raps a groan coming from a window where some boarder had turned over in his sleep and a corncob in the mattress had raked him crossways.

There was one old chap that we'll call Dillaway—Ebenezer Dillaway. That wan't his name; his real one's too well known to tell. He runs the "Dillaway Combination Stores" that are all over the country. In them stores you can buy anything and buy it cheap—cheapness is Ebenezer's stronghold and job lots is his sheet anchor. He'll sell you a mowing machine and the grass seed to grow the hay to cut with it. He'll sell you a suit of clothes for two dollars and a quarter, and for ten cents more he'll sell you glue enough to stick it together again after you've worn it out in the rain. He'll sell you anything, and he's got cash enough to sink a ship.

He come to the "Old Home House" with his daughter, and he took to the place right away. Said 'twas for all the world like where he used to live when he was a boy. He liked the grub and he liked the cornhusks and he liked Brown. Brown had a way of stealing a thing and yet paying enough for it to square the law—that hit Ebenezer where he lived.

His daughter liked Brown, too, and 'twas easy enough to see that Brown liked her. She was a mighty pretty girl, the kind Peter called a "queen," and the active manager took to her like a cat to a fish. They was together more'n half the time, gitting up sailing parties, or playing croquet, or setting up on the "Lover's Nest," which was a kind of slab summer-house Brown had rigged up on the bluff where Aunt Sophrony's pig-pens used to be in the old days.

Me and Jonadab see how things was going, and we'd look at one another and wink and shake our heads when the pair'd go by together. But all that was afore the count come aboard.

We got our first letter from the count about the third of June. The writing was all over the plate like a biled dinner, and the English looked like it had been shook up in a bag, but it was signed with a nine fathom, toggle-jinted name that would give a pollparrot the lockjaw, and had the word "Count" on the bow of it.

You never see a feller happier than Peter T. Brown.

"Can he have rooms?" says Peter. "*Can* he? Well, I should rise to elocute! He can have the best there is if yours truly has to bunk in the coop with the gladsome Plymouth Rock. That's what! He says he's a count and he'll be advertised as a count from this place to where rolls the Oregon."

And he was, too. The papers was full of how

Count What's-his-Name was hanging out at the "Old Home House," and we got more letters from rich old women and pork-pickling money bags than you could shake a stick at. If you want to catch the free and equal nabob of a glorious republic, bait up with a little nobility and you'll have your salt wet in no time. We had to rig up rooms in the carriage house, and me and Jonadab slept in the haymow.

The count himself hove in sight on June fifteenth. He was a little, smoked Italian man with a pair of legs that would have been carried away in a gale, and a black mustache with waxed ends that you'd think would punch holes in the pillow case. His talk was like his writing, only worse, but from the time his big trunk with the foreign labels was carried upstairs, he was skipper and all hands of the "Old Home House."

And the funny part of it was that old man Dillaway was as much gone on him as the rest. For a self-made American article he was the worst gone on this machine-made importation that ever you see. I s'pose when you've got more money than you can spend for straight goods you nat'rally go in for buying curiosities; I can't see no other reason.

Anyway, from the minute the count come over the side it was "Good-by, Peter." The foreigner

was first oar with the old man and general con-
sort for the daughter. Whenever there was a
sailing trip on or a spell of roosting in the Lover's
Nest, Ebenezer would see that the count looked
out for the "queen," while Brown stayed on
the piazza and talked bargains with papa. It
worried Peter—you could see that. He'd set in
the barn with Jonadab and me, thinking, thinking, and all at once he'd bust out:

"Bless that Dago's heart! I haven't chummed
in with the degenerate aristocracy much in my
time, but somewhere or other I've seen that chap
before. Now where—where—where?"

For the first two weeks the count paid his board
like a major; then he let it slide. Jonadab
and me was a little worried, but he was advertising us like fun, his photographs—snap shots
by Peter—was getting into the papers, so we
judged he was a good investment. But Peter
got bluer and bluer.

One night we was in the setting room—me and
Jonadab and the count and Ebenezer. The
"queen" and the rest of the boarders was abed.

The count was spinning a pigeon English
yarn of how he'd fought a duel with rapiers.
When he'd finished, old Dillaway pounded his
knee and sung out:

"That's bus'ness! That's the way to fix 'em!

No lawsuits, no argument, no delays. Just take
'em out and punch holes in 'em. Did you hear
that, Brown ? "

"Yes, I heard it," says Peter, kind of absent-
minded like. "Fighting with razors, wan't it ? "

Now there wan't nothing to that—'twas just
some of Brown's sarcastic spite getting the best
of him—but I give you my word that the count
turned yellow under his brown skin, kind of
like mud rising from the bottom of a pond.

"What-a you say ? " he says, bending for'ards.

"Mr. Brown was mistaken, that's all," says
Dillaway; "he meant rapiers."

"But why-a razors—why-a razors ? " says the
count.

Now I was watching Brown's face, and all at
once I see it light up like you'd turned a search-
light on it. He settled back in his chair and
fetched a long breath as if he was satisfied. Then
he grinned and begged pardon and talked a blue
streak for the rest of the evening.

Next day he was the happiest thing in sight,
and when Miss Dillaway and the count went
Lover's Nesting he didn't seem to care a bit.
All of a sudden he told Jonadab and me that he
was going up to Boston that evening on bus'ness
and wouldn't be back for a day or so. He wouldn't
tell what the bus'ness was, either, but just whis-

tled and laughed and sung, "Good-by, Susannah; don't you grieve for me," till train time.

He was back again three nights afterward, and he come right out to the barn without going nigh the house. He had another feller with him, a kind of shabby dressed Italian man with curly hair.

"Fellers," he says to me and Jonadab, "this is my friend, Mr. Macaroni; he's going to engineer the barber shop for a while."

Well, we'd just let our other barber go, so we didn't think anything of this, but when he said that his friend Spaghetti was going to stay in the barn for a day or so, and that we needn't mention that he was there, we thought that was funny.

But Peter done a lot of funny things the next day. One of 'em was to set a feller painting a side of the house by the count's window, that didn't need painting at all. And when the feller quit for the night, Brown told him to leave the ladder where 'twas.

That evening the same crowd was together in the setting room. Peter was as lively as a cricket, talking, talking, all the time. By and by he says:

"Oh, say, I want you to see the new barber. He can shave anything from a note to a porkypine. Come in here, Chianti!" he says, opening the door and calling out. "I want you."

And in come the new Italian man, smiling and bowing and looking "meek and lowly, sick and sore," as the song says.

Well, we laughed at Brown's talk and asked the Italian all kinds of fool questions and nobody noticed that the count wan't saying nothing. Pretty soon he gets up and says he guesses he'll go to his room, 'cause he feels sort of sick.

And I tell you he looked sick. He was yellower than he was the other night, and he walked like he hadn't got his sea legs on. Old Dillaway was terrible sorry and kept asking if there wan't something he could do, but the count put him off and went out.

"Now that's too bad!" says Brown. "Spaghetti, you needn't wait any longer."

So the other Italian went out, too.

And then Peter T. Brown turned loose and talked the way he done when me and Jonadab first met him. He just spread himself. He told of this bargain that he'd made and that sharp trade he had turned, while we set there and listened and laughed like a parsel of fools. And every time that Ebenezer'd get up to go to bed, Peter'd trot out a new yarn and he'd have to stop to listen to that. And it got to be eleven o'clock and then twelve and then one.

It was just about quarter past one and we was

laughing our heads off at one of Brown's jokes, when out under the back window there was a jingle and a thump and a kind of groaning and wiggling noise.

"What on earth is that?" says Dillaway.

"I shouldn't be surprised," says Peter, cool as a mack'rel on ice, "if that was his royal highness, the count."

He took up the lamp and we all hurried outdoors and 'round the corner. And there, sure enough, was the count, sprawling on the ground with his leather satchel alongside of him, and his foot fast in a big steel trap that was hitched by a chain to the lower round of the ladder. He rared up on his hands when he see us and started to say something about an outrage.

"Oh, that's all right, your majesty," says Brown. "Hi, Chianti, come here a minute! Here's your old college chum, the count, been and put his foot in it."

When the new barber showed up the count never made another move, just wilted like a morning-glory after sunrise. But you never see a worse upset man than Ebenezer Dillaway.

"But what does this mean?" says he, kind of wild like. "Why don't you take that thing off his foot?"

"Oh," says Peter, "he's been elongating my

pedal extremity for the last month or so; I don't see why I should kick if he pulls his own for a while. You see," he says, "it's this way:

"Ever since his grace condescended to lend the glory of his countenance to this humble roof,"

HE RARED UP ON HIS HANDS.

he says, "it's stuck in my mind that I'd seen the said countenance somewhere before. The other night when our conversation was trifling with the razor subject and the Grand Lama here"—that's the name he called the count—"was throwing in details about his carving his friends, it flashed across me where I'd seen it. About a couple of years ago I was selling the guileless rural druggists contiguous to Scranton, Pennsylvania, the tasty and happy combination called 'Dr. Bulger's Electric Liver Cure,' the same being a sort of electric light for shady livers, so to speak. I made my headquarters at Scranton, and, while there, my hair was shortened and my chin smoothed in a neat but gaudy barber shop, presided over by my friend Spaghetti here, and my equally valued friend the count."

"So," says Peter, smiling and cool as ever, "when it all came back to me, as the song says, I journeyed to Scranton accompanied by a photograph of his lordship. I was lucky enough to find Macaroni in the same old shop. He knew the count's classic profile at once. It seems his majesty had hit up the lottery a short time previous for a few hundred and had given up barbering. I suppose he'd read in the papers that the imitation count line was stylish and profitable and so he tried it on. It may be," says Brown, offhand, "that he thought he might marry some rich girl. There's some fool fathers, judging by the papers, that are willing to sell their daughters for the proper kind of tag on a package like him."

Old man Dillaway kind of made a face, as if he'd ate something that tasted bad, but he didn't speak.

"And so," says Peter, "Spaghetti and I came to the Old Home together, he to shave for twelve per, and I to set traps, etcetera. That's a good trap," he says, nodding, "I bought it in Boston. I had the teeth filed down, but the man that sold it said 'twould hold a horse. I left the ladder by his grace's window, thinking he might find it handy after he'd seen his friend of other days, particularly as the back door was locked.

"And now," goes on Brown, short and sharp, "let's talk business. Count," he says, "you are set back on the books about sixty odd for old home comforts. We'll cut off half of that and charge it to advertising. You draw well, as the man said about the pipe. But the other thirty you'll have to work out. You used to shave like a bird. I'll give you twelve dollars a week to chip in with Macaroni here and barber the boarders."

But Dillaway looked anxious.

"Look here, Brown," he says, "I wouldn't do that. I'll pay his board bill and his traveling expenses if he clears out this minute. It seems tough to set him shaving after he's been such a big gun around here."

I could see right off that the arrangement suited Brown first rate and was exactly what he'd been working for, but he pretended not to care much for it.

"Oh! I don't know," he says. "I'd rather be a sterling barber than a plated count. But anything to oblige you, Mr. Dillaway."

So the next day there was a nobleman missing at the "Old Home House," and all we had to remember him by was a trunk full of bricks. And Peter T. Brown and the "queen" was roosting in the Lover's Nest; and the new Italian was busy in the barber shop. He could shave, too. He shaved me without a pull, and my face ain't no plush sofy, neither.

And before the season was over the engagement was announced. Old Dillaway took it pretty well, considering. He liked Peter, and his having no money to speak of didn't count, because Ebenezer had enough for all hands. The old man said he'd been hoping for a son-in-law sharp enough to run the "Consolidated Stores" after he was gone, and it looked, he said, as if he'd found him.

THE SOUTH SHORE WEATHER BUREAU

THE SOUTH SHORE WEATHER BUREAU

"But," says Cap'n Jonadab and me together, jest as if we was "reading in concert" same as the youngsters do in school, "but," we says, "will it work? Will anybody pay for it?"

"Work?" says Peter T., with his fingers in the arm-holes of the double-breasted danger-signal that he called a vest, and with his cigar tilted up till you'd think 'twould set his hat-brim afire. "Work?" says he. "Well, maybe 'twouldn't work if the ordinary brand of canned lobster was running it, but with *me* to jerk the lever and sound the loud timbrel—why, say! it's like stealing money from a blind cripple that's hard of hearing."

"Yes, I know," says Cap'n Jonadab. "But this ain't like starting the Old Home House. That was opening up a brand-new kind of hotel that nobody ever heard of before. This is peddling weather prophecies when there's the Gov'-ment Weather Bureau running opposition—not to mention the Old Farmer's Almanac, and I don't know how many more," he says.

Brown took his patent leathers down off the rail of the piazza, give the ashes of his cigar a flip —he knocked 'em into my hat that was on the floor side of his chair, but he was too excited to mind—and he says:

"Confound it, man!" he says. "You can throw more cold water than a fire-engine. Old Farmer's Almanac! This isn't any 'About this time look out for snow' business. And it ain't any Washington cold slaw like 'Weather for New England and Rocky Mountains, Tuesday to Friday; cold to warm; well done on the edges with a rare streak in the middle, preceded or followed by rain, snow, or clearing. Wind, north to south, varying east and west.' No siree! this is *to-day's* weather on Cape Cod, served right off the griddle on a hot plate, and cooked by the chef a that. You don't realize what a regular dime-museum wonder the feller is," he says.

Well, I suppose we didn't. You see, Jonadab and me, and the rest of the folks around Wellmouth, have come to take Beriah Crocker and his weather forcast as the regular thing, like baked beans on a Saturday night. Beriah, he——

But there! I've been sailing stern first. Let's get her headed right, if we ever expect to turn the first mark. You see, 'twas this way:

'Twas in the early part of May follering the year

that the "Old Home House" was opened. We'd had the place all painted up, decks holy-stoned, bunks overhauled, and one thing or 'nother, and the "Old Home" was all taut and shipshape, ready for the crew—boarders, I mean. Passages was booked all through the summer and it looked as if our second season would be better'n our first.

Then the Dillaway girl—she was christened Lobelia, like her mother, but she'd painted it out and cruised under the name of Belle since the family got rich—she thought 'twould be nice to have what she called a "spring house-party" for her particular friends 'fore the regular season opened. So Peter—he being engaged at the time and consequent in that condition where he'd have put on horns and "mooed" if she'd give the order—he thought 'twould be nice, too, and for a week it was "all hands on deck!" getting ready for the "house-party."

Two days afore the thing was to go off the ways Brown gets a letter from Belle, and in it says she's invited a whole lot of folks from Chicago and New York and Boston and the land knows where, and that they've never been to the Cape and she wants to show 'em what a "quaint" place it is. "Can't you get," says she, "two or three delightful, queer, old 'longshore characters to be at work 'round the hotel? It'll give such a touch of local color," she says.

So out comes Peter with the letter.

"Barzilla," he says to me, "I want some characters. Know anybody that's a character?"

"Well," says I, "there's Nate Slocum over to Orham. He'd steal anything that wa'n't spiked down. He's about the toughest character I can think of, offhand, this way."

"Oh, thunder!" says Brown. "I don't want a crook; that wouldn't be any novelty to *this* crowd," he says. "What I'm after is an odd stick; a feller with pigeons in his loft. Not a lunatic, but jest a queer genius—little queerer than you and the Cap'n here."

After a while we got his drift, and I happened to think of Beriah and his chum, Eben Cobb. They lived in a little shanty over to Skakit P'int and got their living lobstering, and so on. Both of 'em had saved a few thousand dollars, but you couldn't get a cent of it without giving 'em ether, and they'd rather live like Portugees than white men any day, unless they was paid to change. Beriah's pet idee was foretelling what the weather was going to be. And he could do it, too, better'n anybody I ever see. He'd smell a storm further'n a cat can smell fish, and he hardly ever made a mistake. Prided himself on it, you understand, like a boy does on his first long pants. His prophecies was his idols, so's to speak, and you couldn't have hired him to foretell what he knew was wrong, not for no money.

Peter said Beriah and Eben was just the sort of "cards" he was looking for and drove right over to see 'em. He hooked 'em, too. I knew he would; he could talk a Come-Outer into believing that a Unitarian wasn't booked for Tophet, if he set out to.

So the special train from Boston brought the "house-party" down, and our two-seated buggy brought Beriah and Eben over. They didn't have anything to do but to look "picturesque" and say "I snum!" and "I swan to man!" and they could do that to the skipper's taste. The city folks thought they was "just too dear and odd for anything," and made 'em bigger fools than ever, which wa'n't necessary.

The second day of the "party" was to be a sailing trip clear down to the life-saving station on Setuckit Beach. It certainly looked as if 'twas going to storm, and the Gov'ment predictions said it was, but Beriah said "No," and stuck out that 'twould clear up by and by. Peter wanted to know what I thought about their starting, and I told him that 'twas my experience that where weather was concerned Beriah was a good, safe anchorage. So they sailed away, and, sure enough, it cleared up fine. And the next day the Gov'ment fellers said "clear" and Beriah said "rain," and she poured a flood. And, after three or four of such experiences, Beriah was all hunky with the "house-party," and they looked at him as a sort of wonderful freak, like a two-headed calf or the "snake child," or some such outrage.

So, when the party was over, 'round comes Peter, busting with a new notion. What he cal'lated to do was to start a weather prophesying bureau all on his own hook, with Beriah for prophet, and him for manager and general advertiser, and Jonadab and me to help put up the money to get her going. He argued that summer folks from Scituate to Provincetown, on both sides of the Cape, would pay good prices for the real thing in weather predictions. The Gov'ment bureau, so he said, covered too much ground, but Beriah was local and hit her right on the head. His idee was to send Beriah's predictions by telegraph to agents in every Cape town each morning, and the agents was to hand 'em to susscribers. First week a free trial; after that, so much per prophecy.

And it worked—oh, land, yes! it worked. Peter's letters and circulars would satisfy anybody that black was white, and the free trial was a sure bait. I don't know why 'tis, but if you offered the smallpox free, there'd be a barrel of victims waiting in line to come down with it. Brown rigged up a little shanty on the bluff in front of the "Old Home," and filled it full of barometers and thermometers and chronometers and charts, and put Beriah and Eben inside to look wise and make b'lieve do something. That was the office of "The South Shore Weather Bureau," and 'twas sort of sacred and holy, and 'twould kill you to see the boarders tip-toeing up and peeking in the winder to watch them two old coots squinting through a telescope at the sky or scribbling rubbish on paper. And Beriah was right 'most every time. I don't know why— my notion is that he was born that way, same as some folks are born lightning calculators—but I'll never forget the first time Peter asked him how he done it.

"Wall," drawls Beriah, "now to-day looks fine and clear, don't it? But last night my left elbow had rheumatiz in it, and this morning my bones ache, and my right toe-j'int is sore, so I know we'll have an easterly wind and rain this evening. If it had been my left toe now, why——"

Peter held up both hands.

"That'll do," he says. "I ain't asking any

more questions. *Only,* if the boarders or outsiders
ask you how you work it, you cut out the bones
and toe business and talk science and tempera-
ture to beat the cars. Understand, do you? It's
science or no eight-fifty in the pay envelope. Left
toe-joint!" And he goes off grinning.

We had to have Eben, though he wasn't wuth
a green hand's wages as a prophet. But him
and Beriah stuck by each other like two flies in
the glue-pot, and you couldn't hire one without
t'other. Peter said 'twas all right—two prophets
looked better'n one, anyhow; and, as subscrip-
tions kept up pretty well, and the Bureau paid a
fair profit, Jonadab and me didn't kick.

In July, Mrs. Freeman—she had charge of
the upper decks in the "Old Home" and was
rated head chambermaid—up and quit, and
being as we couldn't get another capable Cape
Codder just then, Peter fetched down a woman
from New York; one that a friend of old Dillaway's recommended. She was able seaman so
far's the work was concerned, but she'd been
good-looking once and couldn't forget it, and
she was one of them clippers that ain't happy
unless they've got a man in tow. You know the
kind: pretty nigh old enough to be a coal-barge,
but all rigged up with bunting and frills like a
yacht.

Her name was Kelly, Emma Kelly, and she was a widow—whether from choice or act of Providence I don't know. The other women servants was all down on her, of course, 'cause she had city ways and a style of wearing her togs that made their Sunday gowns and bonnets look like distress signals. But they couldn't deny that she was a driver so far's her work was concerned. She'd whoop through the hotel like a no'theaster and have everything done, and done well, by two o'clock in the afternoon. Then she'd be ready to dress up and go on parade to astonish the natives.

Men—except the boarders, of course—was scarce around Wellmouth Port. First the Kelly lady begun to flag Cap'n Jonadab and me, but we sheered off and took to the offing. Jonadab, being a widower, had had his experience, and I never had the marrying disease and wasn't hankering to catch it. So Emma had to look for other victims, and the prophet-shop looked to her like the most likely feeding-ground.

And, would you b'lieve it, them two old critters, Beriah and Eben, gobbled the bait like sculpins. If she'd been a woman like the kind they was used to—the Cape kind, I mean—I don't s'pose they'd have paid any attention to her; but she was diff'rent from anything they'd ever run up against, and the first thing you know, she had 'em both poke-hooked. 'Twas all in fun on her part first along, I cal'late, but pretty soon some idiot let out that both of 'em was wuth money, and then the race was on in earnest.

She'd drop in at the weather-factory 'long in the afternoon and pretend to be terrible interested in the goings on there.

"I don't see how you two gentlemen *can* tell whether it's going to rain or not. I think you are the most *wonderful* men! Do tell me, Mr. Crocker, will it be good weather to-morrer? I wanted to take a little walk up to the village about four o'clock if it was."

And then Beriah'd swell out like a puffing pig and put on airs and look out of the winder, and crow:

"Yes'm, I jedge that we'll have a southerly breeze in the morning with some fog, but nothing to last, nothing to last. The afternoon, I cal'late, 'll be fair. I—I—that is to say, I was figgering on goin' to the village myself to-morrer."

Then Emma would pump up a blush, and smile, and purr that she was *so* glad, 'cause then she'd have comp'ny. And Eben would glower at Beriah and Beriah'd grin sort of superior-like, and the mutual barometer, so's to speak, would fall about a foot during the next hour. The brotherly business between the two prophets was coming to an end fast, and all on account of Mrs. Kelly.

She played 'em even for almost a month; didn't show no preference one way or the other. First 'twas Eben that seemed to be eating up to wind-'ard, and then Beriah'd catch a puff and gain for a spell. Cap'n Jonadab and me was uneasy, for we was afraid the Weather Bureau would suffer 'fore the thing was done with; but Peter was away, and we didn't like to interfere till he come home.

And then, all at once, Emma seemed to make up her mind, and 'twas all Eben from that time on. The fact is, the widder had learned, some-how or 'nother, that he had the most money of the two. Beriah didn't give up; he stuck to it like a good one, but he was falling behind and he knew it. As for Eben, he couldn't help show-ing a little joyful pity, so's to speak, for his part-ner, and the atmosphere in that rain lab'ratory got so frigid that I didn't know but we'd have to put up a stove. The two wizards was hardly on speaking terms.

The last of August come and the "Old Home House" was going to close up on the day after Labor Day. Peter was down again, and so was Ebenezer and Belle, and there was to be high jinks to celebrate the season's wind-up. There was to be a grand excursion and clambake at Setuckit Beach and all hands was going—four catboats full.

Of course, the weather must be good or it's no joy job taking females to Setuckit in a catboat. The night before the big day, Peter came out to the Weather Bureau and Jonadab and me dropped in likewise. Beriah was there all alone; Eben was out walking with Emma.

"Well, Jeremiah," says Brown, chipper as a mack'rel gull on a spar-buoy, "what's the outlook for to-morrer? The Gov'ment sharp says there's a big storm on the way up from Florida. Is he right, or only an 'also ran,' as usual?"

"Wall," says Beriah, goin' to the door, "I don't know, Mr. Brown. It don't look just right; I swan it don't! I can tell you better in the morning. I hope 'twill be fair, too, 'cause I was cal'lating to get a day off and borrer your horse and buggy and go over to the Ostable campmeeting. It's the big day over there," he says.

Now, I knew of course, that he meant he was going to take the widder with him, but Peter spoke up and says he:

"Sorry, Beriah, but you're too late. Eben asked me for the horse and buggy this morning. I told him he could have the open buggy; the other one's being repaired, and I wouldn't lend the new surrey to the Grand Panjandrum himself. Eben's going to take the fair Emma for a ride," he says. "Beriah, I'm afraid our beloved Cobb is, in the innocence of his youth, being roped in by the sophisticated damsel in the shoo-fly hat," says he.

Me and Jonadab hadn't had time to tell Peter how matters stood betwixt the prophets, or most likely he wouldn't have said that. It hit Beriah like a snowslide off a barn roof. I found out afterwards that the widder had more'n half promised to go with *him*. He slumped down in his chair as if his mainmast was carried away, and he didn't even rise to blow for the rest of the time we was in the shanty. Just set there, looking fishy-eyed at the floor.

Next morning I met Eben prancing around in his Sunday clothes and with a necktie on that would make a rainbow look like a mourning badge.

"Hello!" says I. "You seem to be pretty chipper. You ain't going to start for that fifteen-mile ride through the woods to Ostable, be you? Looks to me as if 'twas going to rain."

"The predictions for this day," says he, "is cloudy in the forenoon, but clearing later on. Wind, sou'east, changing to south and sou'west."

"Did Beriah send that out?" says I, looking doubtful, for if ever it looked like dirty weather, I thought it did right then.

"*Me* and Beriah sent it out," he says, jealous-like. But I knew 'twas Beriah's forecast or he wouldn't have been so sure of it.

Pretty soon out comes Peter, looking dubious at the sky.

"If it was anybody else but Beriah," he says, "I'd say this mornings prophecy ought to be sent to *Puck*. Where is the seventh son of the seventh son—the only original American seer?"

He wasn't in the weather-shanty, and we finally found him on one of the seats 'way up on the edge of the bluff. He didn't look 'round when we come up, but just stared at the water.

"Hey, Elijah!" says Brown. He was always calling Beriah "Elijah" or "Isaiah" or "Jeremiah" or some other prophet name out of Scripture. "Does this go?" And he held out the telegraph-blank with the morning's prediction on it.

Beriah looked around just for a second. He looked to me sort of sick and pale—that is, as pale as his sun-burned rhinoceros hide would ever turn.

"The forecast for to-day," says he, looking at the water again, "is cloudy in the forenoon,

but clearing later on. Wind sou'east, changing
to south and sou'west."

"Right you are!" says Peter, joyful. "We
start for Setuckit, then. And here's where the
South Shore Weather Bureau hands another
swift jolt to your Uncle Sam."

So, after breakfast, the catboats loaded up, the
girls giggling and screaming, and the men boarders dressed in what they hoped was sea-togs.
They sailed away 'round the lighthouse and
headed up the shore, and the wind was sou'east
sure and sartin, but the "clearing" part wasn't
in sight yet.

Beriah didn't watch 'em go. He stayed in the
shanty. But by and by, when Eben drove the
buggy out of the barn and Emma come skipping
down the piazza steps, I see him peeking out of
the little winder.

The Kelly critter had all sail sot and colors
flying. Her dress was some sort of mosquito
netting with wall-paper posies on it, and there was
more ribbons flapping than there is reef-p'ints
on a mainsail. And her hat! Great guns! It
looked like one of them pictures you see in a
flower-seed catalogue.

"Oh!" she squeals, when she sees the buggy.
"Oh! Mr. Cobb. Ain't you afraid to go in
that open carriage? It looks to me like rain."

But Eben waved his flipper, scornful. "My forecast this morning," says he, "is cloudy now, but clearing by and by. You trust to me, Mis' Kelly. Weather's my business."

"Of *course* I trust you, Mr. Cobb," she says, "Of course I trust you, but I should hate to spile my gown, that's all."

They drove out of the yard, fine as fiddlers, and I watched 'em go. When I turned around, there was Beriah watching 'em too, and he was smiling for the first time that morning. But it was one of them kind of smiles that makes you wish he'd cry.

At ha'f-past ten it begun to sprinkle; at eleven 'twas raining hard; at noon 'twas a pouring, roaring, sou'easter, and looked good for the next twelve hours at least.

"Good Lord! Beriah," says Cap'n Jonadab, running into the Weather Bureau, "you've missed stays *this* time, for sure. Has your prophecy-works got indigestion?" he says.

But Beriah wasn't there. The shanty was closed, and we found out afterwards that he spent that whole day in the store down at the Port.

By two o'clock 'twas so bad that I put on my ileskins and went over to Wellmouth and tele-phoned to the Setuckit Beach life-saving station to find out if the clambakers had got there right side up. They'd got there; fact is, they was in the station then, and the language Peter hove through that telephone was enough to melt the wires. 'Twas all in the shape of compliments to the prophet, and I heard Central tell him she'd report it to the head office. Brown said 'twas blowing so they'd have to come back by the inside channel, and that meant landing 'way up Harniss way, and hiring teams to come to the Port with from there.

'Twas nearly eight when they drove into the yard and come slopping up the steps. And *such* a passel of drownded rats you never see. The women-folks made for their rooms, but the men hopped around the parlor, shedding puddles with every hop, and hollering for us to trot out the head of the Weather Bureau.

"Bring him to me," orders Peter, stopping to pick his pants loose from his legs; "I yearn to caress him."

And what old Dillaway said was worse'n that.

But Beriah didn't come to be caressed. 'Twas quarter past nine when we heard wheels in the yard.

"By mighty!" yells Cap'n Jonadab; "it's the camp-meeting pilgrims. I forgot them. Here's a snow."

He jumped to open the door, but it opened afore he got there and Beriah come in. He didn't pay no attention to the welcome he got from the gang, but just stood on the sill, pale, but grinning the grin that a terrier dog has on just as you're going to let the rat out of the trap.

Somebody outside says: "Whoa, consarn you!" Then there was a thump and a sloshy stamping on the steps, and in comes Eben and the widder.

I had one of them long-haired, foreign cats once that a British skipper gave me. 'Twas a yeller and black one and it fell overboard. When we fished it out it looked just like the Kelly woman done then. Everybody but Beriah just screeched —we couldn't help it. But the prophet didn't laugh; he only kept on grinning.

Emma looked once round the room, and her eyes, as well as you could see 'em through the snarl of dripping hair and hat-trimming, fairly snapped. Then she went up the stairs three steps at a time.

Eben didn't say a word. He just stood there and leaked. Leaked and smiled. Yes, sir! his face, over the mess that had been that rainbow necktie, had the funniest look of idiotic joy on it that ever *I* see. In a minute everybody else shut up. We didn't know what to make of it.

'Twas Beriah that spoke first.

"He! he! he!" he chuckled. "He! he! he! Wasn't it kind of wet coming through the woods, Mr. Cobb? What does Mrs. Kelly think of the day her beau picked out to go to camp-meeting in?"

Then Eben came out of his trance.

IN COMES EBEN AND THE WIDDER.

"Beriah," says he, holding out a dripping flipper, "shake!"

But Beriah didn't shake. Just stood still.

"I've got a s'prise for you, shipmate," goes on Eben. "Who did you say that lady was ? "

Beriah didn't answer. I begun to think that some of the wet had soaked through the assistant prophet's skull and had give him water on the brain.

"You called her Mis' Kelly, didn't you ? " gurgled Eben. "Wall, that ain't her name. Her and me stopped at the Baptist parsonage over to East Harniss when we was on the way home and got married. She's Mis' Cobb now," he says.

Well, the queerest part of it was that 'twas the bad weather was really what brought things to a head so sudden. Eben hadn't spunked up anywhere nigh enough courage to propose, but they stopped at Ostable so long, waiting for the rain to let up, that 'twas after dark when they was half way home. Then Emma—oh, she was a slick one!—said that her reputation would be ruined, out that way with a man that wa'n't her husband. If they was married now, she said— and even a dummy could take *that* hint.

I found Beriah at the weather-shanty about an hour afterwards with his head on his arms. He looked up when I come in.

"Mr. Wingate," he says, "I'm a fool, but for the land's sake don't think I'm *such* a fool as not to know that this here storm was bound to strike to-day. I lied," he says; "I lied about the weather for the first time in my life; lied right up and down so as to get her mad with him. My repertation's gone forever. There's a feller in the Bible that sold his—his birthday, I think 'twas—for a mess of porridge. I'm him; only," and he groaned awful, "they've cheated me out of the porridge."

But you ought to have read the letters Peter got next day from subscribers that had trusted to the prophecy and had gone on picnics and such like. The South Shore Weather Bureau went out of business right then.

THE DOG STAR

THE DOG STAR

It commenced the day after we took old man Stumpton out codfishing. Me and Cap'n Jonadab both told Peter T. Brown that cod wa'n't biting much at that season, but he said cod be jiggered.

"What's troubling me just now is landing suckers," he says.

So the four of us got into the *Patience M.*— she's Jonadab's catboat—and sot sail for the Crab Ledge. And we hadn't more'n got our lines over the side than we struck into a school of dogfish. Now, if you know anything about fishing you know that when the dogfish strike on it's "good-by, cod!" So when Stumpton hauled a big fat one over the rail I could tell that Jonadab was ready to swear. But do you think it disturbed your old friend, Peter Brown? No, sir! He never winked an eye.

"By Jove!" he sings out, staring at that dogfish as if 'twas a gold dollar. "By Jove!" says he, "that's the finest specimen of a Labrador

77

mack'rel ever I see. Bait up, Stump, and go at 'em again.''

So Stumpton, having lived in Montana ever sence he was five years old, and not having sighted salt water in all that time, he don't know but what there *is* such critters as "Labrador mack'rel," and he goes at 'em, hammer and tongs. When we come ashore we had eighteen dogfish, four sculpin and a skate, and Stumpton was the happiest loon in Ostable County. It was all we could do to keep him from cooking one of them "mack'-rel" with his own hands. If Jonadab hadn't steered him out of the way while I sneaked down to the Port and bought a bass, we'd have had to eat dogfish—we would, as sure as I'm a foot high.

Stumpton and his daughter, Maudina, was at the Old Home House. 'Twas late in September, and the boarders had cleared out. Old Dilla-way—Peter's father-in-law—had decoyed the pair on from Montana because him and some Wall Street sharks were figgering on buying some copper country out that way that Stumpton owned. Then Dillaway was took sick, and Peter, who was just back from his wedding tower, brought the Montana victims down to the Cape with the ex-cuse to give 'em a good time alongshore, but really to keep 'em safe and out of the way till

Ebenezer got well enough to finish robbing 'em. Belle—Peter's wife—stayed behind to look after papa.

Stumpton was a great tall man, narrer in the beam, and with a figgerhead like a henhawk. He enjoyed himself here at the Cape. He fished, and loafed, and shot at a mark. He sartinly could shoot. The only thing he was wishing for was something alive to shoot at, and Brown had promised to take him out duck shooting. 'Twas too early for ducks, but that didn't worry Peter any; he'd a-had ducks to shoot at if he bought all the poultry in the township.

Maudina was like her name, pretty, but sort of soft and mushy. She had big blue eyes and a baby face, and her principal cargo was poetry. She had a deckload of it, and she'd heave it overboard every time the wind changed. She was forever ordering the ocean to "roll on," but she didn't mean it; I had her out sailing once when the bay was a little mite rugged, and I know. She was just out of a convent school, and you could see she wasn't used to most things—including men.

The first week slipped along, and everything was serene. Bulletins from Ebenezer more encouraging every day, and no squalls in sight. But 'twas almost too slick. I was afraid the calm was a weather breeder, and sure enough, the hurricane struck us the day after that fishing trip.

Peter had gone driving with Maudina and her dad, and me and Cap'n Jonadab was smoking on the front piazza. I was pulling at a pipe, but the cap'n had the home end of one of Stumpton's cigars harpooned on the little blade of his jackknife, and was busy pumping the last drop of comfort out of it. I never see a man who wanted to get his money's wuth more'n Jonadab, I give you my word, I expected to see him swaller that cigar remnant every minute.

And all to once he gives a gurgle in his throat.

"Take a drink of water," says I, scared like.

"Well, by time!" says he, pointing.

A feller had just turned the corner of the house and was heading up in our direction. He was a thin, lengthy craft, with more'n the average amount of wrists sticking out of his sleeves, and with long black hair trimmed aft behind his ears and curling on the back of his neck. He had high cheek bones and kind of sunk-in black eyes, and altogether he looked like "Dr. Macgoozleum, the Celebrated Blackfoot Medicine Man." If he'd hollered: "Sagwa Bitters, only one dollar a bottle!" I wouldn't have been surprised.

But his clothes—don't say a word! His coat

was long and buttoned up tight, so's you couldn't
tell whether he had a vest on or not—though
'twas a safe bet he hadn't—and it and his pants
was made of the loudest kind of black-and-white
checks. No nice quiet pepper-and-salt, you understand, but the checkerboard kind, the oilcloth
kind, the kind that looks like the marble floor
in the Boston post-office. They was pretty
tolerable seedy, and so was his hat. Oh, he was
a last year's bird's nest *now*, but when them clothes
was fresh—whew! the northern lights and a
rainbow mixed wouldn't have been more'n a
cloudy day 'longside of him.

He run up to the piazza like a clipper coming
into port, and he sweeps off that rusty hat and
hails us grand and easy.

"Good-morning, gentlemen," says he.

"We don't want none," says Jonadab, decided.

The feller looked surprised. "I beg your pardon," says he. "You don't want any—what?"

"We don't want any 'Life of King Solomon'
nor 'The World's Big Classifyers.' And we don't
want to buy any patent paint, nor sewing ma-
chines, nor clothes washers, nor climbing ever-
green roses, nor rheumatiz salve. And we don't
want our pictures painted, neither."

Jonadab was getting excited. Nothing riles

him wuss than a peddler, unless it's a woman selling tickets to a church fair. The feller swelled up until I thought the top button on that thunderstorm coat would drag anchor, sure.

"You are mistaken," says he. "I have called to see Mr. Peter Brown; he is—er—a relative of mine."

Well, you could have blown me and Jonadab over with a cat's-paw. We went on our beam ends, so's to speak. A relation of Peter T.'s; why, if he'd been twice the panorama he was we'd have let him in when he said that. Loud clothes, we figgered, must run in the family. We remembered how Peter was dressed the first time we met him.

"You don't say!" says I. "Come right up and set down, Mr.—Mr.——"

"Montague," says the feller. "Booth Montague. Permit me to present my card."

He drove into the hatches of his checkerboards and rummaged around, but he didn't find nothing but holes, I jedge, because he looked dreadful put out, and begged our pardons five or six times.

"Dear me!" says he. "This is embarassing. I've forgot my cardcase."

We told him never mind the card; any of Peter's folks was more'n welcome. So he come up the steps and set down in a piazza chair like

King Edward perching on his throne. Then he hove out some remarks about its being a nice morning, all in a condescending sort of way, as if he usually attended to the weather himself, but had been sort of busy lately, and had handed the job over to one of the crew. We told him all about Peter, and Belle, and Ebenezer, and about Stumpton and Maudina. He was a good deal interested, and asked consider'ble many questions. Pretty soon we heard a carriage rattling up the road.

"Hello!" says I. "I guess that's Peter and the rest coming now."

Mr. Montague got off his throne kind of sudden.

"Ahem!" says he. "Is there a room here where I may—er—receive Mr. Brown in a less public manner? It will be rather a—er—surprise for him, and——"

Well, there was a good deal of sense in that. I know 'twould surprise *me* to have such an image as he was sprung on me without any notice. We steered him into the gents' parlor, and shut the door. In a minute the horse and wagon come into the yard. Maudina said she'd had a "heavenly" drive, and unloaded some poetry concerning the music of billows and pine trees, and such. She and her father went up to their rooms, and when the decks was clear Jonadab and me tackled Peter T.

"Peter," says Jonadab, "we've got a surprise for you. One of your relations has come."

Brown, he did look surprised, but he didn't act as he was any too joyful.

"Relation of *mine?*" says he. "Come off! What's his name?"

We told him Montague, Booth Montague. He laughed.

"Wake up and turn over," he says. "They never had anything like that in my family. Booth Montague! Sure 'twa'n't Algernon Cough-drops?"

We said no, 'twas Booth Montague, and that he was waiting in the gents' parlor. So he laughed again, and said somethin' about sending for Laura Lean Jibbey, and then we started.

The checkerboard feller was standing up when we opened the door. "Hello, Petey!" says he, cool as a cucumber, and sticking out a foot and a half of wrist with a hand at the end of it.

Now, it takes considerable to upset Peter Theodosius Brown. Up to that time and hour I'd have bet on him against anything short of an earthquake. But Booth Montague done it —knocked him plumb out of water. Peter actually turned white.

"Great——" he began, and then stopped and

swallered. "*Hank!*" he says, and set down in a chair.

"The same," says Montague, waving the starboard extension of the checkerboard. "Petey, it does me good to set my eyes on you. Especially now, when you're the real thing."

Brown never answered for a minute. Then he canted over to port and reached down into his pocket. "Well," says he, "how much?"

But Hank, or Booth, or Montague—whatever his name was—he waved his flipper disdainful. "Nun-nun-nun-no, Petey, my son," he says, smiling. "It ain't 'how much?' this time. When I heard how you'd rung the bell the first shot out the box and was rolling in coin, I said to myself: 'Here's where the prod comes back to his own.' I've come to live with you, Petey, and you pay the freight."

Peter jumped out of the chair. "*Live* with me!" he says. "You Friday evening amateur night! It's back to 'Ten Nights in a Barroom' for yours!" he says.

"Oh, no, it ain't!" says Hank, cheerful. "It'll be back to Popper Dillaway and Belle. When I tell 'em I'm your little cousin Henry and how you and me worked the territories together— why—well, I guess there'll be gladness round the dear home nest; hey?"

Peter didn't say nothing. Then he fetched a long breath and motioned with his head to Cap'n Jonadab and me. We see we weren't invited to the family reunion, so we went out and shut the door. But we did pity Peter; I snum if we didn't!

It was most an hour afore Brown come out of that room. When he did he took Jonadab and me by the arm and led us out back of the barn.

"Fellers," he says, sad and mournful, "that —that plaster cast in a crazy-quilt," he says, referring to Montague, "is a cousin of mine. That's the living truth," says he, "and the only excuse I can make is that 'tain't my fault. He's my cousin, all right, and his name's Hank Schmults, but the sooner you box that fact up in your forgetory, the smoother 'twill be for yours drearily, Peter T. Brown. He's to be Mr. Booth Montague, the celebrated English poet, so long's he hangs out at the Old Home; and he's to hang out here until—well, until I can dope out a way to get rid of him."

We didn't say nothing for a minute—just thought. Then Jonadab says, kind of puzzled: "What makes you call him a poet?" he says.

Peter answered pretty snappy: "'Cause there's only two or three jobs that a long-haired image like him could hold down," he says. "I'd call him a musician if he could play 'Bedelia' on a jews'-harp; but he can't, so's he's got to be a poet."

And a poet he was for the next week or so. Peter drove down to Wellmouth that night and bought some respectable black clothes, and the follering morning, when the celebrated Booth Montague come sailing into the dining room, with his curls brushed back from his forehead, and his new cutaway on, and his wrists covered up with clean cuffs, blessed if he didn't look distinguished—at least, that's the only word I can think of that fills the bill. And he talked beautiful language, not like the slang he hove at Brown and us in the gents' parlor.

Peter done the honors, introducing him to us and the Stumptons as a friend who'd come from England unexpected, and Hank he bowed and scraped, and looked absent-minded and crazy— like a poet ought to. Oh, he done well at it! You could see that 'twas just pie for him.

And 'twas pie for Maudina, too. Being, as I said, kind of green concerning men folks, and likewise taking to poetry like a cat to fish, she just fairly gushed over this fraud. She'd reel off a couple of fathom of verses from fellers named Spencer or Waller, or such like, and he'd never turn a hair, but back he'd come and say they was good, but he preferred Confucius, or Methuselah, or somebody so antique that she nor nobody else ever heard of 'em. Oh, he run a safe course, and he had *her* in tow afore they turned the first mark.

Jonadab and me got worried. We see how things was going, and we didn't like it. Stumpton was having too good a time to notice, going after "Labrador mack'rel" and so on, and Peter T. was too busy steering the cruises to pay any attention. But one afternoon I come by the summerhouse unexpected, and there sat Booth Montague and Maudina, him with a clove hitch round her waist, and she looking up into his eyes like they were peekholes in the fence 'round paradise. That was enough. It just simply *couldn't* go any further, so that night me and Jonadab had a confab up in my room.

"Barzilla," says the cap'n, "if we tell Peter that that relation of his is figgering to marry Maudina Stumpton for her money, and that he's more'n likely to elope with her, 'twill pretty nigh kill Pete, won't it? No, sir; it's up to you and me. We've got to figger out some way to get rid of the critter ourselves."

"It's a wonder to me," I says, "that Peter puts up with him. Why don't he order him to clear out, and tell Belle if he wants to? She can't blame Peter 'cause his uncle was father to an outrage like that."

Jonadab looks at me scornful. "Can't, hey?" he says. "And her high-toned and chumming in with the bigbugs? It's easy to see you never was married," says he.

Well, I never was, so I shut up.

We set there and thought and thought, and by and by I commenced to sight an idee in the offing. 'Twas hull down at first, but pretty soon I got it into speaking distance, and then I broke it gentle to Jonadab. He grabbed at it like the "Labrador mack'rel" grabbed Stumpton's hook. We set up and planned until pretty nigh three o'clock, and all the next day we put in our spare time loading provisions and water aboard the *Patience M*. We put grub enough aboard to last a month.

Just at daylight the morning after that we knocked at the door of Montague's bedroom. When he woke up enough to open the door— it took some time, 'cause eating and sleeping was his mainstay—we told him that we was planning an early morning fishing trip, and if he wanted to go with the folks he must come down to the landing quick. He promised to hurry, and I stayed by the door to see that he didn't get away.

In about ten minutes we had him in the skiff rowing off to the *Patience M.*

"Where's the rest of the crowd?" says he, when he stepped aboard.

"They'll be along when we're ready for 'em," says I. "You go below there, will you, and stow away the coats and things."

So he crawled into the cabin, and I helped Jonadab get up sail. We intended towing the skiff, so I made her fast astern. In half a shake we was under way and headed out of the cove. When that British poet stuck his nose out of the companion we was abreast the p'int.

"Hi!" says he, scrambling into the cockpit. "What's this mean?"

I was steering and feeling toler'ble happy over the way things had worked out.

"Nice sailing breeze, ain't it?" says I, smiling.

"Where's Mau—Miss Stumpton?" he says, wild like.

"She's abed, I cal'late," says I, "getting her beauty sleep. Why don't *you* turn in? Or are you pretty enough now?"

He looked first at me and then at Jonadab, and his face turned a little yellower than usual.

"What kind of a game is this?" he asks, brisk. "Where are you going?"

'Twas Jonadab that answered. " We're

bound," says he, "for the Bermudas. It's a lovely place to spend the winter, they tell me," he says.

That poet never made no remarks. He jumped to the stern and caught hold of the skiff's painter. I shoved him out of the way and picked up the boat hook. Jonadab rolled up his shirt sleeves and laid hands on the centerboard stick.

"I wouldn't, if I was you," says the cap'n.

Jonadab weighs pretty close to two hundred, and most of it's gristle. I'm not quite so much, fur's tonnage goes, but I ain't exactly a canary bird. Montague seemed to size things up in a jiffy. He looked at us, then at the sail, and then at the shore out over the stern.

"Done!" says he. "Done! And by a couple of 'farmers'!"

And down he sets on the thwart.

Well, we sailed all that day and all that night. 'Course we didn't really intend to make the Bermudas. What we intended to do was to cruise around alongshore for a couple of weeks, long enough for the Stumptons to get back to Dillaway's, settle the copper business and break for Montana. Then we was going home again and turn Brown's relation over to him to take care of. We knew Peter'd have some plan thought out by that time. We'd left a note telling him what we'd done, and saying that we trusted to him to explain matters to Maudina and her dad. We knew that explaining was Peter's main holt.

The poet was pretty chipper for a spell. He set on the thwart and bragged about what he'd do when he got back to "Petey" again. He said we couldn't git rid of him so easy. Then he spun yarns about what him and Brown did when they was out West together. They was interesting yarns, but we could see why Peter wa'n't anxious to introduce Cousin Henry to Belle. Then the *Patience M.* got out where 'twas pretty rugged, and she rolled consider'ble and after that we didn't hear much more from friend Booth—he was too busy to talk.

That night me and Jonadab took watch and watch. In the morning it thickened up and looked squally. I got kind of worried. By nine o'clock there was every sign of a no'theaster, and we see we'd have to put in somewheres and ride it out. So we headed for a place we'll call Baytown, though that wa'n't the name of it. It's a queer, old-fashioned town, and it's on an island; maybe you can guess it from that.

Well, we run into the harbor and let go anchor. Jonadab crawled into the cabin to get some ter-backer, and I was for'ard coiling the throat hal-yard. All at once I heard oars rattling, and I turned my head; what I see made me let out a yell like a siren whistle.

There was that everlasting poet in the skiff —you remember we'd been towing it astern— and he was jest cutting the painter with his jack-knife. Next minute he'd picked up the oars and was heading for the wharf, doubling up and stretching out like a frog swimming, and with his curls streaming in the wind like a rooster's tail in a hurricane, He had a long start 'fore Jonadab and me woke up enough to think of chasing him.

But we woke up fin'lly, and the way we flew round that catboat was a caution. I laid into them halyards, and I had the mainsail up to the peak afore Jonadab got the anchor clear of the bottom. Then I jumped to the tiller, and the *Patience M.* took after that skiff like a pup after a tomcat. We run alongside the wharf just as Booth Hank climbed over the stringpiece.

"Get after him, Barzilla!" hollers Cap'n Jonadab. "I'll make her fast."

Well, I hadn't took more'n three steps when I see 'twas goin' to be a long chase. Montague unfurled them thin legs of his and got over the ground something wonderful. All you could see was a pile of dust and coat tails flapping.

Up on the wharf we went and round the corner into a straggly kind of road with old-fashioned houses on both sides of it. Nobody in the yards, nobody at the windows; quiet as could be, except that off ahead, somewheres, there was music playing.

That road was a quarter of a mile long, but we galloped through it so fast that the scenery was nothing but a blur. Booth was gaining all the time, but I stuck to it like a good one. We took a short cut through a yard, piled over a fence and come out into another road, and up at the head of it was a crowd of folks—men and women and children and dogs.

"Stop thief!" I hollers, and 'way astern I heard Jonadab bellering: "Stop thief!"

Montague dives headfirst for the crowd. He fell over a baby carriage, and I gained a tack 'fore he got up. He wa'n't more'n ten yards ahead when I come busting through, upsetting children and old women, and landed in what I guess was the main street of the place and right abreast of a parade that was marching down the middle of it.

First there was the band, four fellers tooting and banging like fo'mast hands on a fishing smack in a fog. Then there was a big darky toting a banner with "Jenkins' Unparalleled Double Uncle Tom's Cabin Company, No. 2,"

on it in big letters. Behind him was a boy leading two great, savage looking dogs—bloodhounds,
I found out afterwards—by chains. Then come
a pony cart with Little Eva and Eliza's child in
it; Eva was all gold hair and beautifulness.
And astern of her was Marks the Lawyer, on his
donkey. There was lots more behind him, but
these was all I had time to see just then.

Now, there was but one way for Booth Hank
to get acrost that street, and that was to bust
through the procession. And, as luck would
have it, the place he picked out to cross was just
ahead of the bloodhounds. And the first thing I
knew, them dogs stretched out their noses and took
a long sniff, and then bust out howling like all
possessed. The boy, he tried to hold 'em, but
'twas no go. They yanked the chains out of his
hands and took after that poet as if he owed 'em
something. And every one of the four million
other dogs that was in the crowd on the sidewalks
fell into line, and such howling and yapping and
scampering and screaming you never heard.

Well, 'twas a mixed-up mess. That was the end
of the parade. Next minute I was racing across
country with the whole town and the Uncle Tom-
mers astern of me, and a string of dogs stretched out
ahead fur's you could see. 'Way up in the lead
was Booth Montague and the bloodhounds, and

away aft I could hear Jonadab yelling: "Stop thief!"

'Twas lively while it lasted, but it didn't last long. There was a little hill at the end of the field, and where the poet dove over 'tother side of it the bloodhounds all but had him. Afore I got to the top of the rise I heard the awfullest powwow going on in the holler, and thinks I: "*They're eating him alive!*"

But they wan't. When I hove in sight Montague was setting up on the ground at the foot of the sand bank he'd fell into, and the two hounds was rolling over him, lapping his face and going on as if he was their grandpa jest home from sea with his wages in his pocket. And round them, in a double ring, was all the town dogs, crazy mad, and barking and snarling, but scared to go any closer.

In a minute more the folks begun to arrive; boys first, then girls and men, and then the women. Marks came trotting up, pounding the donkey with his umbrella.

"Here, Lion! Here, Tige!" he yells. "Quit it! Let him alone!" Then he looks at Montague, and his jaw kind of drops.

"Why—why, *Hank!*" he says.

A tall, lean critter, in a black tail coat and a yaller vest and lavender pants, comes puffing up. He was the manager, we found out afterward.

"Have they bit him ?" says he. Then he done just the same as Marks; his mouth opened and

"THEY'RE EATING HIM ALIVE!"

his eyes stuck out. "*Hank Schmults*, by the living jingo!" says he.

Booth Montague looks at the two of 'em kind of sick and lonesome. "Hello, Barney! How are you, Sullivan?" he says.

I thought 'twas about time for me to get prominent. I stepped up, and was just going to say something when somebody cuts in ahead of me.

"Hum!" says a voice, a woman's voice, and

tolerable crisp and vinegary. "Hum! it's you, is it? I've been looking for *you!*"

'Twas Little Eva in the pony cart. Her lovely posy hat was hanging on the back of her neck, her gold hair had slipped back so's you could see the black under it, and her beautiful red cheeks was kind of streaky. She looked some older and likewise mad.

"Hum!" says she, getting out of the cart. "It's you, is it, Hank Schmults? Well, p'r'aps you'll tell me where you've been for the last two weeks? What do you mean by running away and leaving your——"

Montague interrupted her. "Hold on, Maggie, hold on!" he begs. "*Don't* make a row here. It's all a mistake; I'll explain it to you all right. Now, please——"

"Explain!" hollers Eva, kind of curling up her fingers and moving toward him. "Explain, will you? Why, you miserable, low-down——"

But the manager took hold of her arm. He'd been looking at the crowd, and I cal'late he saw that here was the chance for the best kind of an advertisement. He whispered in her ear. Next thing I knew she clasped her hands together, let out a scream and runs up and grabs the celebrated British poet round the neck.

"Booth!" says she. "My husband! Saved! Saved!"

And she went all to pieces and cried all over his necktie. And then Marks trots up the child, and that young one hollers: "Papa! papa!" and tackles Hank around the legs. And I'm blessed if Montague don't slap his hand to his forehead, and toss back his curls, and look up at the sky, and sing out: "My wife and babe! Restored to me after all these years! The heavens be thanked!"

Well, 'twas a sacred sort of time. The town folks tiptoed away, the men looking solemn but glad, and the women swabbing their deadlights and saying how affecting 'twas, and so on. Oh, you could see that show would do business *that* night, if it never did afore.

The manager got after Jonadab and me later on, and did his best to pump us, but he didn't find out much. He told us that Montague belonged to the Uncle Tom's Cabin Company, and that he'd disappeared a fortni't or so afore, when they were playing at Hyannis. Eva was his wife, and the child was their little boy. The bloodhounds knew him, and that's why they chased him so.

"What was you two yelling 'Stop thief!' after him for?" says he. "Has he stole anything?"

We says "No."

"Then what did you want to get him for?" he says.

"We didn't," says Jonadab. "We wanted to get rid of him. We don't want to see him no more."

You could tell that the manager was puzzled, but he laughed.

"All right," says he. "If I know anything about Maggie—that's Mrs. Schmults—he won't get loose ag'in."

We only saw Montague to talk to but once that day. Then he peeked out from under the winder shade at the hotel and asked us if we'd told anybody where he'd been. When he found we hadn't, he was thankful.

"You tell Petey," says he, "that he's won the whole pot, kitty and all. I don't think I'll visit him again, nor Belle, neither."

"I wouldn't," says I. "They might write to Maudina that you was a married man. And old Stumpton's been praying for something alive to shoot at," I says.

The manager gave Jonadab and me a couple of tickets, and we went to the show that night. And when we saw Booth Hank Montague parading about the stage and defying the slave hunters, and telling 'em he was a free man, standing on the Lord's free soil, and so on, we realized 'twould have been a crime to let him do anything else.

"As an imitation poet," says Jonadab, "he was a kind of mildewed article, but as a play actor—well, there may be some that can beat him, but I never see 'em!"

THE MARE AND THE MOTOR

THE MARE AND THE MOTOR

Them Todds had got on my nerves. 'Twas Peter's ad that brought 'em down. You see, 'twas 'long toward the end of the season at the Old Home, and Brown had been advertising in the New York and Boston papers to "bag the leftovers," as he called it. Besides the reg'lar hogwash about the "breath of old ocean" and the "simple, cleanly living of the bygone days we dream about," there was some new froth concerning hunting and fishing. You'd think the wild geese roosted on the flagpole nights, and the bluefish clogged up the bay so's you could walk on their back fins without wetting your feet—that is, if you wore rubbers and trod light.

"There!" says Peter T., waving the advertisement and crowing gladsome; "they'll take to that like your temp'rance aunt to brandy cough-drops. We'll have to put up barbed wire to keep 'em off."

"Humph!" grunts Cap'n Jonadab. "Anybody but a born fool'll know there ain't any shooting down here this time of year."

Peter looked at him sorrowful. "Pop," says he, "did you ever hear that Solomon answered a summer hotel ad? This ain't a Chautauqua, this is the Old Home House, and its motto is: 'There's a new victim born every minute, and there's twenty-four hours in a day.' You set back and count the clock ticks."

Well, that's 'bout all we had to do. We got boarders enough from that ridiculous advertisement to fill every spare room we had, including Jonadab's and mine. Me and the cap'n had to bunk in the barn loft; but there was some satisfaction in that—it give us an excuse to get away from the "sports" in the smoking room.

The Todds was part of the haul. He was a little, dried-up man, single, and a minister. Nigh's I could find out, he'd given up preaching by the request of the doctor and his last congregation. He had a notion that he was a mighty hunter afore the Lord, like Nimrod in the Bible, and he'd come to the Old Home to bag a few gross of geese and ducks.

His sister was an old maid, and slim, neither of which failings was from choice, I cal'late. She wore eye-glasses and a veil to "preserve her complexion," and her idee seemed to be that native Cape Codders lived in trees and ate cocoanuts. She called 'em "barbarians, utter barbarians."

Whenever she piped "James" her brother had to drop everything and report on deck. She was skipper of the Todd craft.

Them Todds was what Peter T. called "the limit, and a chip or two over." The other would-be gunners and fishermen were satisfied to slam shot after sandpeeps, or hook a stray sculpin or a hake. But t'wa'n't so with brother James Todd and sister Clarissa. "Ducks" it was in the advertising, and nothing *but* ducks they wanted. Clarissa, she commenced to hint middling p'inted concerning fraud.

Finally we lost patience, and Peter T., he said they'd got to be quieted somehow, or he'd do some shooting on his own hook; said too much Toddy was going to his head. Then I suggested taking 'em down the beach somewheres on the chance of seeing a stray coot or loon or something—*anything* that could be shot at. Jonadab and Peter agreed 'twas a good plan, and we matched to see who'd be guide. And I got stuck, of course; my luck again.

So the next morning we started, me and the Reverend James and Clarissa in the *Greased Lightning*, Peter's new motor launch. First part of the trip that Todd man done nothing but ask questions about the launch; I had to show him how to start it and steer it, and the land knows

what all. Clarissa set around doing the heavy con-
temptuous and turning up her nose at creation
generally. It must have its drawbacks, this
roosting so fur above the common flock; seems
to me I'd be thinking all the time of the bump
that was due me if I got shoved off the perch.

Well, by and by Lonesome Huckleberries'
shanty hove in sight, and I was glad to see it,
although I had to answer a million questions
about Lonesome and his history.

I told the Todds that, so fur as nationality was
concerned he was a little of everything, like a
picked-up dinner; principally Eyetalian and
Portugee, I cal'late, with a streak of Gay Head
Injun. His real name's long enough to touch
bottom in the ship channel at high tide, so folks
got to calling him "Huckleberries" because he
peddles them kind of fruit in summer. Then
he mopes around so with nary a smile on his
face, that it seemed right to tack on the "Lonesome." So "Lonesome Huckleberries" he's been
for ten years. He lives in the patchwork shanty
on the beach down there, he is deaf and dumb,
drives a liver-colored, balky mare that no one
but himself and his daughter Becky can handle,
and he has a love for bad rum and a temper that's
landed him in the Wellmouth lock-up more than
once or twice. He's one of the best gunners

alongshore and at this time he owned a flock of
live decoys that he'd refused as high as fifteen
dollars apiece for. I told all this and a lot more.

When we struck the beach, Clarissa, she took
her paint box and umbrella and mosquito 'intment, and the rest of her cargo, and went off by
herself to "sketch." She was great on "sketch-
ing," and the way she'd use up good paint and
spile nice clean paper was a sinful waste. Afore
she went, she give me three fathom of sailing
orders concerning taking care of "James." You'd
think he was about four year old; made me feel
like a hired nurse.

James and me went perusing up and down
that beach in the blazing sun looking for something to shoot. We went 'way beyond Lonesome's
shanty, but there wa'n't nobody to home. Lonesome himself, it turned out afterward, was up to
the village with his horse and wagon, and his
daughter Becky was over in the wood, on the
mainland berrying. Todd was a cheerful talker,
but limited. His favorite remark was: "Oh,
I say, my deah man." That's what he kept
calling me, "my deah man." Now, my name
ain't exactly a Claude de Montmorency for pret-
tiness, but "Barzilla" 'll fetch *me* alongside a good
deal quicker'n "my deah man," I'll tell you that.

We frogged it up and down all the forenoon,

but didn't git a shot at nothing but one stray "squawk" that had come over from the Cedar Swamp. I told James 'twas a canvasback, and he blazed away at it, but missed it by three fathom, as might have been expected.

Finally, my game leg—rheumatiz, you understand—begun to give out. So I flops down in the shade of a sand bank to rest, and the reverend goes poking off by himself.

I cal'late I must have fell asleep, for when I looked at my watch it was close to one o'clock, and time for us to be getting back to port. I got up and stretched and took an observation, but further'n Clarissa's umbrella on the skyline, I didn't see anything stirring. Brother James wa'n't visible, but I jedged he was within hailing distance. You can't see very fur on that point, there's too many sand hills and hummocks.

I started over toward the *Greased Lightning*. I'd gone only a little ways, and was down in a gully between two big hummocks, when "Bang! bang!" goes both barrels of a shotgun, and that Todd critter busts out hollering like all possessed.

"'Hooray!'" he squeals, in that squeaky voice of his. "Hooray! I've got 'em! I've got 'em!"

Thinks I, "What in the nation does the lunatic cal'late he's shot?" And I left my own gun laying where 'twas and piled up over the edge of that sand bank like a cat over a fence. And then I see a sight.

There was James, hopping up and down in the beach grass, squealing like a Guinea hen with a sore throat, and waving his gun with one wing— arm, I mean—and there in front of him, in the foam at the edge of the surf, was two ducks as dead as Nebuchadnezzar—two of Lonesome Huckleberries' best decoy ducks—ducks he'd tamed and trained, and thought more of than anything else in this world—except rum, maybe —and the rest of the flock was digging up the beach for home as if they'd been telegraped for, and squawking "Fire!" and "Murder!"

Well, my mind was in a kind of various state, as you might say, for a minute. 'Course, I'd known about Lonesome's owning them decoys —told Todd about 'em, too—but I hadn't seen 'em nowhere alongshore, and I sort of cal'lated they was locked up in Lonesome's hen house, that being his usual way when he went to town. I s'pose likely they'd been feeding among the beach grass somewheres out of sight, but I don't know for sartin to this day. And I didn't stop to reason it out then, neither. As Scriptur' or George Washin'ton or somebody says, "'twas a condition, not a theory," I was afoul of.

"I've got 'em!" hollers Todd, grinning till I

thought he'd swaller his own ears. "I shot 'em all myself!"

"You everlasting——" I begun, but I didn't get any further. There was a rattling noise behind me, and I turned, to see Lonesome Huckleberries himself, setting on the seat of his old truck wagon and glaring over the hammer head of that balky mare of his straight at brother Todd and the dead decoys.

For a minute there was a kind of tableau, like them they have at church fairs—all four of us, including the mare, keeping still, like we was frozen. But 'twas only for a minute. Then it turned into the liveliest moving picture that ever *I* see. Lonesome couldn't swear—being a dummy —but if ever a man got profane with his eyes, he did right then. Next thing I knew he tossed both hands into the air, clawed two handfuls out of the atmosphere, reached down into the cart, grabbed a pitch-fork and piled out of that wagon and after Todd. There was murder coming and I could see it.

"Run, you loon!" I hollers, desperate.

James didn't wait for any advice. He didn't know what he'd done, I cal'late, but he jedged 'twas his move. He dropped his gun and put down the shore like a wild man, with Lonesome after him. I tried to foller, but my rheumatiz was too big a handicap; all I could do was yell.

You never'd have picked out Todd for a sprinter —not to look at him, you wouldn't—but if he didn't beat the record for his class just then I'll eat my sou'wester. He fairly flew, but Lonesome split tacks with him every time, and kept to wind'ard, into the bargain. When they went out of sight amongst the sand hills 'twas anybody's race.

I was scart. I knew what Lonesome's temper was, 'specially when it had been iled with some Wellmouth Port no-license liquor. He'd been took up once for half killing some boys that tormented him, and I figgered if he got within pitchfork distance of the Todd critter he'd make him the leakiest divine that ever picked a text. I commenced to hobble back after my gun. It looked bad to me.

But I'd forgot sister Clarissa. 'Fore I'd limped fur I heard her calling to me.

"Mr. Wingate," says she, "get in here at once."

There she was, setting on the seat of Lonesome's wagon, holdin' the reins and as cool as a white frost in October.

"Get in at once," says she. I jedged 'twas good advice, and took it.

"Proceed," says she to the mare. "Git dap!" says I, and we started. When we rounded the sand hill we see the race in the distance. Lonesome had gained a p'int or two, and Todd wa'n't more'n four pitchforks in the lead.

"Make for the launch!" I whooped, between my hands.

The parson heard me and come about and broke for the shore. The *Greased Lightning* had swung out about the length of her anchor rope, and the water wa'n't deep. Todd splashed in to his waist and climbed aboard. He cut the roding just as Lonesome reached tide mark. James, he sees it's a close call, and he shins back to the engine, reaching it exactly at the time when the gent with the pitchfork laid hands on the rail. Then the parson throws over the switch—I'd shown him how, you remember—and gives the starting wheel a full turn.

Well, you know the *Greased Lightning?* She don't linger to say farewell, not any to speak of, she don't. And this time she jumped like the cat that lit on the hot stove. Lonesome, being balanced with his knees on the rail, pitches headfust into the cockpit. Todd, jumping out of his way, falls overboard backward. Next thing anybody knew, the launch was scooting for blue water like a streak of what she was named for, and the hunting chaplain was churning up foam like a mill wheel.

I yelled more orders than second mate on a coaster. Todd bubbled and bellered. Lonesome hung on to the rail of the cockpit and let his hair stand up to grow. Nobody was cool but

HE PITCHED HEAD FIRST INTO THE COCKPIT.

Clarissa, and she was an iceberg. She had her good p'ints, that old maid did, drat her!

"James," she calls, "get out of that water this minute and come here! This instant, mind!"

James minded. He paddled ashore and hopped,

dripping like a dishcloth, alongside the truck wagon.

"Get in!" orders Skipper Clarissa. He done it. "Now," says the lady, passing the reins over to me, "drive us home, Mr. Wingate, before that intoxicated lunatic can catch us."

It seemed about the only thing to do. I knew 'twas no use explaining to Lonesome for an hour or more yet, even if you can talk finger signs, which part of my college training has been neglected. 'Twas murder he wanted at the present time. I had some sort of a foggy notion that I'd drive along, pick up the guns and then get the Todds over to the hotel, afterward coming back to get the launch and pay damages to Huckleberries. I cal'lated he'd be more reasonable by that time.

But the mare had made other arrangements. When I slapped her with the end of the reins she took the bit in her teeth and commenced to gallop. I hollered "Whoa!" and "Heave to!" and "Belay!" and everything else I could think of, but she never took in a reef. We bumped over hummocks and ridges, and every time we done it we spilled something out of that wagon. First 'twas a lot of huckleberry pails, then a basket of groceries and such, then a tin pan with some potatoes in it, then a jug done up in a blanket. We was heaving cargo overboard like a leaky ship in a typhoon. Out of the tail of my eye I see Lonesome, well out to sea, heading the *Greased Lightning* for the beach.

Clarissa put in the time soothing James, who had a serious case of the scart-to-deaths, and calling me an "utter barbarian" for driving so fast. Lucky for all hands, she had to hold on tight to keep from being jounced out, 'long with the rest of movables, so she couldn't take the reins. As for me, I wa'n't paying much attention to her —'twas the Cut-Through that was disturbing *my* mind.

When you drive down to Lonesome P'int you have to ford the "Cut-Through." It's a strip of water between the bay and the ocean, and 'tain't very wide nor deep at low tide. But the tide was coming in now, and, more'n that, the mare wa'n't headed for the ford. She was cuttin' cross-lots on her own hook, and wouldn't answer the helm.

We struck that Cut-Through about a hundred yards east of the ford, and in two shakes we was hub deep in salt water. 'Fore the Todds could do anything but holler the wagon was afloat and the mare was all but swimming. But she kept right on. Bless her, you *couldn't* stop her!

We crossed the first channel and come out on a flat where 'twasn't more'n two foot deep then. I commenced to feel better. There was another channel ahead of us, but I figured we'd navigate that same as we had the first one. And then the most outrageous thing happened.

If you'll b'lieve it, that pesky mare balked and wouldn't stir another step.

And there we was! I punched and kicked and hollered, but all that stubborn horse would do was lay her ears back flat, and snarl up her lip, and look round at us, much as to say: "Now, then, you land sharks, I've got you between wind and water!" And I swan to man if it didn't look as if she had!

"Drive on!" says Clarissa, pretty average vinegary. "Haven't you made trouble enough for us already, you dreadful man? Drive on!"

Hadn't *I* made trouble enough! What do you think of that?

"You want to drown us!" says Miss Todd, continuing her chatty remarks. "I see it all! It's a plot between you and that murderer. I give you warning; if we reach the hotel, my brother and I will commence suit for damages."

My temper's fairly long-suffering, but 'twas raveling some by this time.

"Commence suit!" I says. "I don't care *what* you commence, if you'll commence to keep quiet now!" And then I give her a few p'ints as to what her brother had done, heaving in some personal flatteries every once in a while for good measure.

I'd about got to thirdly when James give a screech and p'inted. And, if there wa'n't Lonesome in the launch, headed right for us, and coming a-b'iling! He'd run her along abreast of the beach and turned in at the upper end of the Cut-Through.

You never in your life heard such a row as there was in that wagon. Clarissa and me yelling to Lonesome to keep off—forgitting that he was stone deaf and dumb—and James vowing that he was going to be slaughtered in cold blood. And the *Greased Lightning* p'inted just so she'd split that cart amidships, and coming—well, you know how she can go.

She never budged until she was within ten foot of the flat, and then she sheered off and went past in a wide curve, with Lonesome steering with one hand and shaking his pitchfork at Todd with t'other. And *such* faces as he made-up! They'd have got him hung in any court in the world.

He run up the Cut-Through a little ways, and then come about, and back he comes again, never slacking speed a mite, and running close to the shoal as he could shave, and all the time going through the bloodiest kind of pantomimes. And past he goes, to wheel 'round and commence all over again.

Thinks I, "Why don't he ease up and lay us aboard? He's got all the weapons there is. Is he scart?"

And then it come to me—the reason why. *He didn't know how to stop her.* He could steer first rate, being used to sailboats, but an electric auto launch was a new ideal for him, and he didn't understand her works. And he dastn't run her aground at the speed she was making; 'twould have finished her and, more'n likely, him, too.

I don't s'pose there ever was another mess just like it afore or sence. Here was us, stranded with a horse we couldn't make go, being chased by a feller who was run away with in a boat he couldn't stop!

Just as I'd about give up hope, I heard somebody calling from the beach behind us. I turned, and there was Becky Huckleberries, Lonesome's daughter. She had the dead decoys by the legs in one hand.

"Hi!" says she.

"Hi!" says I. "How do you get this giraffe of yours under way?"

She held up the decoys.

"Who kill-a dem ducks?" says she.

I p'inted to the reverend. "He did," says I. And then I cal'late I must have had one of them things they call an inspiration. "And he's willing to pay for 'em, I says.

"Pay thirty-five dolla?" says she.

"You bet!" says I.

But I'd forgot Clarissa. She rose up in that waterlogged cart like a Statue of Liberty. "Never!" says she. "We will never submit to such extortion. We'll drown first!"

Becky heard her. She didn't look disapp'inted nor nothing. Just turned and begun to walk up the beach. "*All* right," says she; "*goo'*-by."

The Todds stood it for a jiffy. Then James give in. "I'll pay it!" he hollers. "I'll pay it!"

Even then Becky didn't smile. She just come about again and walked back to the shore. Then she took up that tin pan and one of the potaters we'd jounced out of the cart.

"Hi, Rosa!" she hollers. That mare turned her head and looked. And, for the first time sence she hove anchor on that flat, the critter unfurled her ears and histed 'em to the masthead.

"Hi, Rosa!" says Becky again, and begun to pound the pan with the potater. And I give you my word that that mare started up, turned the wagon around nice as could be, and begun to swim ashore. When we got where the critter's legs touched bottom, Becky remarks: "Whoa!"

"Here!" I yells, "what did you do that for?"

"Pay thirty-five dolla *now*," says she. She was bus'ness, that girl.

Todd got his wallet from under hatches and counted out the thirty-five, keeping one eye on Lonesome, who was swooping up and down in the launch looking as if he wanted to cut in, but dasn't. I tied the bills to my jack-knife, to give 'em weight, and tossed the whole thing ashore. Becky, she counted the cash and stowed it away in her apron pocket.

"*All* right," says she. "Hi, Rosa!" The potater and pan performance begun again, and Rosa picked up her hoofs and dragged us to dry land. And it sartinly felt good to the feet

"Say," I says, "Becky, it's none of my affairs, as I know of, but is that the way you usually start that horse of yours?"

She said it was. And Rosa ate the potater.

Becky asked me how to stop the launch, and I told her. She made a lot of finger signs to Lonesome, and inside of five minutes the *Greased Lightning* was anchored in front of us. Old man Huckleberries was still hankering to interview Todd with the pitchfork, but Becky settled that all right. She jumped in front of him, and her eyes snapped and her feet stamped and her fingers flew. And 'twould have done you good to see her dad shrivel up and get humble. I always had thought that a woman wasn't much good as a boss of the roost unless she could use her tongue, but Becky showed me my mistake. Well, it's live and l'arn.

Then Miss Huckleberries turned to us and smiled.

"*All* right," says she; "*goo'*-by."

Them Todds took the train for the city next morning. I drove 'em to the depot. James was kind of glum, but Clarissa talked for two. Her opinion of the Cape and Capers, 'specially me, was decided. The final blast was just as ¬he was climbing the car steps.

"Of all the barbarians," says she; "utter, uncouth, murdering barbarians in——"

She stopped, thinking for a word, I s'pose. I didn't feel that I could improve on Becky Huckleberries conversation much, so I says:

"*All* right! *Goo'*-by!"

THE MARK ON THE DOOR

THE MARK ON THE DOOR

One nice moonlight evening me and Cap'n Jonadab and Peter T., having, for a wonder, a little time to ourselves and free from boarders, was setting on the starboard end of the piazza, smoking, when who should heave in sight but Cap'n Eri Hedge and Obed Nickerson. They'd come over from Orham that day on some fish business and had drove down to Wellmouth Port on purpose to put up at the Old Home for the night and shake hands with me and Jonadab. We was mighty glad to see 'em, now I tell you.

They'd had supper up at the fish man's at the Centre, so after Peter T. had gone in and fetched out a handful of cigars, we settled back for a good talk. They wanted to know how business was and we told 'em. After a spell somebody mentioned the Todds and I spun my yarn about the balky mare and the *Greased Lightning*. It tickled 'em most to death, especially Obed.

"Ho, ho!" says he. "That's funny, ain't it. Them power boats are great things, ain't they.

I had an experience in one—or, rather, in two—
a spell ago when I was living over to West Bayport. My doings was with gasoline though, not
electricity. 'Twas something of an experience.
Maybe you'd like to hear it."

"'Way I come to be over there on the bay side
of the Cape was like this. West Bayport, where
my shanty and the big Davidson summer place
and the Saunders' house was, used to be called
Punkhassett—which is Injun for 'The last place
the Almighty made'—and if you've read the
circulars of the land company that's booming
Punkhassett this year, you'll remember that the
principal attraction of them diggings is the 'mag-
nificent water privileges.' 'Twas the water privileges that had hooked me. Clams was thick
on the flats at low tide, and fish was middling
plenty in the bay. I had two weirs set; one a
deep-water weir, a half mile beyond the bar, and
t'other just inside of it that I could drive out to at
low water. A two-mile drive 'twas, too; the tide
goes out a long ways over there. I had a power-
boat—seven and a half power gasoline—that I
kept anchored back of my nighest-in weir in deep
water, and a little skiff on shore to row off to her
in.

"The yarn begins one morning when I went
down to the shore after clams. I'd noticed

the signs then. They was stuck up right acrost the path: 'No trespassing on these premises,' and 'All persons are forbidden crossing this property, under penalty of the law.' But land! I'd used that short-cut ever sence I'd been in Bayport—which was more'n a year—and old man Davidson and me was good friends, so I cal'lated the signs was intended for boys, and hove ahead without paying much attention to 'em. 'Course I knew that the old man—and, what was more important, the old lady—had gone abroad and that the son was expected down, but that didn't come to me at the time, neither.

"I was heading for home about eight, with two big dreeners full of clams, and had just climbed the bluff and swung over the fence into the path, when somebody remarks: 'Here, you!' I jumped and turned round, and there, beating across the field in my direction, was an exhibit which, it turned out later, was ticketed with the name of Alpheus Vandergraff Parker Davidson—'Allie' for short.

"And Allie was a good deal of an exhibit, in his way. His togs were cut to fit his spars, and he carried 'em well—no wrinkles at the peak or sag along the boom. His figurehead was more'n average regular, and his hair was combed real nice—the part in the middle of it looked like it had been laid out with a plumb-line. Also, he had on white shoes and glory hallelujah stockings. Altogether, he was alone with the price of admission, and what some folks, I s'pose, would have called a handsome enough young feller. But I didn't like his eyes; they looked kind of tired, as if they'd seen 'bout all there was to see of some kinds of life. Twenty-four year old eyes hadn't ought to look that way.

"But I wasn't interested in eyes jest then. All I could look at was teeth. There they was, a lovely set of 'em, in the mouth of the ugliest specimen of a bow-legged bulldog that ever tried to hang itself at the end of a chain. Allie was holding t'other end of the chain with both hands, and they were full, at that. The dog stood up on his hind legs and pawed the air with his front ones, and his tongue hung out and dripped. You could see he was yearning, just dying, to taste of a middle-aged longshoreman by the name of Obed Nickerson. I stared at the dog, and he stared at me. I don't know which of us was the most interested.

"'Here, you!' says Allie again. 'What are you crossing this field for?'

"I heard him, but I was too busy counting teeth to pay much attention. 'You ought to feed that dog,' I says, absent-minded like. 'He's hungry.'

"'Humph!' says he. 'Well, maybe he'll be fed in a minute. Did you see those signs?'"

"'Yes,' says I; 'I saw 'em. They're real neat and pretty.'

"'Pretty!' He fairly choked, he was so mad. 'Why, you cheeky, long-legged jay,' he says, 'I'll—— What are you crossing this field for?'

"'So's to get to t'other side of it, I guess,' says I. I was riling up a bit myself. You see, when a feller's been mate of a schooner, like I've been in my day, it don't come easy to be called names. It looked for a minute as if Allie was going to have a fit, but he choked it down.

"'Look here!' he says. 'I know who you are. Just because the gov'ner has been soft enough to let you countrymen walk all over him, it don't foller that I'm going to be. I'm boss here for this summer. My name's——' He told me his name, and how his dad had turned the place over to him for the season, and a lot more. 'I put those signs up,' he says, 'to keep just such fellers as you are off my property. They mean that you ain't to cross the field. Understand?'

"I understood. I was mad clean through, but I'm law-abiding, generally speaking. 'All right,' I says, picking up my dreeners and starting for the farther fence; 'I won't cross it again.'

"'You won't cross it now,' says he. 'Go back where you come from.'

"That was a grain too much. I told him a few things. He didn't wait for the benediction. 'Take him, Prince!' he says, dropping the chain.

HE FAIRLY SOBBED WITH DISAPPOINTMENT.

"Prince was willing. He fetched a kind of combination hurrah and growl and let out for me full-tilt. I don't feed good fresh clams to dogs as a usual thing, but that mouth *had* to be filled. I waited till he was almost on me, and then I let drive with one of the dreeners. Prince and a couple of pecks of clams went up in the air like a busted bomb-shell, and I broke for the fence I'd started for. I hung on to the other dreener, though, just out of principle.

"But I had to let go of it, after all. The dog come out of the collision looking like a plate of scrambled eggs, and took after me harder'n ever, shedding shells and clam juice something scandalous. When he was right at my heels I turned and fired the second dreener. And, by Judas, I missed him!

"Well, principle's all right, but there's times when even the best of us has to hedge. I simply couldn't reach the farther fence, so I made a quick jibe and put for the one behind me. And I couldn't make that, either. Prince was taking mouthfuls of my overalls for appetizers. There was a little pine-tree in the lot, and I give one jump and landed in the middle of it. I went up the rest of the way like I'd forgot something, and then I clung onto the top of that tree and panted and swung round in circles, while the dog hopped up and down on his hind legs and fairly sobbed with disapp'intment.

"Allie was rolling on the grass. 'Oh, *dear* me!' says he, between spasms. 'That was the funniest thing I ever saw.'

"I'd seen lots funnier things myself, but 'twa'n't worth while to argue.   Besides, I was busy hanging onto that tree.   'Twas an awful little pine and the bendiest one I ever climbed.   Allie rolled around a while longer, and then he gets up and comes over.

"'Well, Reuben,' says he, lookin' up at me on the roost, 'you're a good deal handsomer up there than you are on the ground.   I guess I'll let you stay there for a while as a lesson to you.   Watch him, Prince.'   And off he walks.

"'You everlasting clothes-pole,' I yells after him, 'if it wa'n't for that dog of yours I'd——'

"He turns around kind of lazy and says he: 'Oh, you've got no kick coming,' he says.   'I allow you to—er—ornament my tree, and 'tain't every hayseed I'd let do that.'

"And away he goes;   and for an hour that had no less'n sixty thousand minutes in it I clung to that tree like a green apple, with Prince setting open-mouthed underneath waiting for me to get ripe and drop.

"Just as I was figgering that I was growing fast to the limb, I heard somebody calling my name.   I unglued my eyes from the dog and looked up, and there, looking over the fence that I'd tried so hard to reach, was Barbara Saunders,

Cap'n Eben Saunders' girl, who lived in the house next door to mine.

"Barbara was always a pretty girl, and that morning she looked prettier than ever, with her black hair blowing every which way and her black eyes snapping full of laugh. Barbara Saunders in a white shirt-waist and an old, mended skirt could give ten lengths in a beauty race to any craft in silks and satins that ever *I* see, and beat 'em hull down at that.

"'Why, Mr. Nickerson!' she calls. 'What are you doing up in that tree?'

"That was kind of a puzzler to answer offhand, and I don't know what I'd have said if friend Allie hadn't hove in sight just then and saved me the trouble. He come strolling out of the woods with a cigarette in his mouth, and when he saw Barbara he stopped short and looked and looked at her. And for a minute she looked at him, and the red come up in her cheeks like a sunrise.

"'Beg pardon, I'm sure,' says Allie, tossing away the cigarette. 'May I ask if that—er—deep-sea gentleman in my tree is a friend of yours?'

"Barbara kind of laughed and dropped her eyes, and said why, yes, I was.

"'By Jove! he's luckier than I thought,' says Allie, never taking his eyes from her face. 'And what do they call him, please, when they want him to answer?' That's what he asked, though, mind you, he'd said he knew who I was when he first saw me.

"'It's Mr. Nickerson,' says Barbara. 'He lives in that house there. The one this side of ours.'

"'Oh, a neighbor! That's different. Awfully sorry, I'm sure. Prince, come here. Er—Nickerson, for the lady's sake we'll call it off. You may—er—vacate the perch.'

"I waited till he'd got a clove-hitch onto Prince. He had to give him one or two welts over the head 'fore he could do it; the dog acted like he'd been cheated. Then I pried myself loose from that blessed limb and shinned down to solid ground. My! but I was b'iling inside. 'Taint pleasant to be made a show afore folks, but 'twas the feller's condescending what-excuse-you-got-for-living manners that riled me most.

"I picked up what was left of the dreeners and walked over to the fence. That field was just sowed, as you might say, with clams. If they ever sprouted 'twould make a tip-top codfish pasture.

"'You see,' says Allie, talking to Barbara; 'the gov'nor told me he'd been plagued with trespassers, so I thought I'd give 'em a lesson.

But neighbors, when they're scarce as ours are, ought to be friends. Don't you think so, Miss ——? Er—Nickerson,' says he, 'introduce me to our other neighbor.'

"So I had to do it, though I didn't want to. He turned loose some soft soap about not realizing afore what a beautiful place the Cape was. I thought 'twas time to go.

"'But Miss Saunders hasn't answered my question yet,' says Allie. 'Don't *you* think neighbors ought to be friends, Miss Saunders?'

"Barbara blushed and laughed and said she guessed they had. Then she walked away. I started to follow, but Allie stopped me.

"'Look here, Nickerson,' says he. 'I let you off this time, but don't try it again; do you hear?'

"'I hear,' says I. 'You and that hyena of yours have had all the fun this morning. Some day, maybe, the boot'll be on t'other leg.'

"Barbara was waiting for me. We walked on together without speaking for a minute. Then I says, to myself like: 'So that's old man Davidson's son, is it? Well, he's the prize peach in the crate, he is!'

"Barbara was thinking, too. 'He's very nice looking, isn't he?' says she. 'Twas what you'd expect a girl to say, but I hated to hear her say it. I went home and marked a big chalk-mark on the inside of my shanty door, signifying that I had a debt so pay some time or other.

"So that's how I got acquainted with Allie V. P. Davidson. And, what's full as important, that's how he got acquainted with Barbara Saunders.

"Shutting an innocent canary-bird up in the same room with a healthy cat is a more or less risky proposition for the bird. Same way, if you take a pretty country girl who's been to sea with her dad most of the time and tied to the apron-strings of a deef old aunt in a house three miles from nowhere—you take that girl, I say, and then fetch along, as next-door neighbor, a good-looking young shark like Allie, with a hogshead of money and a blame sight too much experience, and that's a risky proposition for the girl.

"Allie played his cards well; he'd set into a good many similar games afore, I judge. He begun by doing little favors for Phœbe Ann—she was the deef aunt I mentioned—and 'twa'n't long afore he was as solid with the old lady as a kedge-anchor. He had a way of dropping into the Saunders house for a drink of water or a slab of 'that delicious apple-pie,' and with every drop he got better acquainted with Barbara. Cap'n Eben was on a v'yage to Buenos Ayres and wouldn't be home till fall, 'twa'n't likely.

"I didn't see a great deal of what was going on, being too busy with my fishweirs and clamming to notice. Allie and me wa'n't exactly David and Jonathan, owing, I judge, to our informal introduction to each other. But I used to see him scooting 'round in his launch—twenty-five foot, she was, with a little mahogany cabin and the land knows what—and the servants at the big house told me yarns about his owning a big steam-yacht, with a sailing-master and crew, which was cruising round Newport somewheres.

"But, busy as I was, I see enough to make me worried. There was a good deal of whispering over the Saunders back gate after supper, and once, when I come up over the bluff from the shore sudden, they was sitting together on a rock and he had his arm round her waist. I dropped a hint to Phœbe Ann, but she shut me up quicker'n a snap-hinge match-box. Allie had charmed 'auntie' all right. And so it drifted along till September.

"One Monday evening about the middle of the month I went over to Phœbe Ann's to borrow some matches. Barbara wasn't in—gone out to lock up the hens, or some such fool excuse. But Phœbe was busting full of joy. Cap'n Eben had arrived in New York a good deal sooner'n was expected and would be home on Thursday morning.

"'He's going from Boston to Provincetown on the steamer, Wednesday,' says Phœbe. 'He's got some business over there. Then he's coming home from Provincetown on the early train. Ain't that splendid?'

"I thought 'twas splendid for more reasons than one, and I went out feeling good. But as I come round the corner of the house there was somebody by the back gate, and I heard a girl's voice sayin': 'Oh, no, no! I can't! I can't!'

"If I hadn't trod on a stick maybe I'd have heard more, but the racket broke up the party. Barbara come hurrying past me into the house, and by the light from the back door, I see her face. 'Twas white as a clam-shell, and she looked frightened to death.

"Thinks I: 'That's funny! It's a providence Eben's coming home so soon.'

"And the next day I saw her again, and she was just as white and wouldn't look me in the eye. Wednesday, though, I felt better, for the servants on the Davidson place told me that Allie had gone to Boston on the morning train to be gone for good, and that they was going to shut up the house and haul up the launch in a day or so.

"Early that afternoon, as I was coming from

my shanty to the bluff on my way to the shore after dinner, I noticed a steam-yacht at anchor two mile or so off the bar. She must have come there sence I got in, and I wondered whose she was. Then I see a dingey with three men aboard rowing in, and I walked down the beach to meet 'em.

"Sometimes I think there is such things as what old Parson Danvers used to call 'dispensations.' This was one of 'em. There was a feller in a uniform cap steering the dingey, and, b'lieve it or not, I'll be everlastingly keelhauled if he didn't turn out to be Ben Henry, who was second mate with me on the old *Seafoam*. He was surprised enough to see me, and glad, too, but he looked sort of worried.

"'Well, Ben,' says I, after we had shook hands, 'well, Ben,' I says, 'my shanty ain't exactly the United States Hotel for gilt paint and bill of fare, but I *have* got eight or ten gallons of home-made cherry rum and some terbacker and an extry pipe. You fall into my wake.'

"'I'd like to, Obed,' he says; 'I'd like to almighty well, but I've got to go up to the store, if there is such a thing in this metropolis, and buy some stuff that I forgot to get in Newport. You see, we got orders to sail in a tearing hurry, and——'

"'Send one of them fo'mast hands to the store,' says I. 'You got to come with me.'

"He hemmed and hawed a while, but he was dry, and I shook the cherry-rum jug at him, figuratively speaking, so finally he give in.

"'You buy so and so,' says he to his men, passing 'em a ten-dollar bill. 'And mind, you don't know nothing. If anybody asks, remember that yacht's the *Mermaid—M-U-R-M-A-D-E*,' he says, 'and she belongs to Mr. Jones, of Mobile, Georgia.'

"So the men went away, and me and Ben headed for my shanty, where we moored abreast of each other at the table, with a jug between us for a buoy, so's to speak. We talked old times and spun yarns, and the tide went out in the jug consider'ble sight faster than 'twas ebbing on the flats. After a spell I asked him about the man that owned the yacht.

"'Who? Oh—er—Brown?' he says. 'Why, he's——'

"'Brown?' says I. 'Thought you said 'twas Jones?'

"Well, that kind of upset him, and he took some cherry-rum to grease his memory. Then I asked more questions and he tried to answer 'em, and got worse tangled than ever. Finally I had to laugh.

"'Look here, Ben,' says I. 'You can't fetch port on that tack. The truth's ten mile astern of you. Who does own that yacht, anyway?'

"He looked at me mighty solemn—cherry-rum solemn. 'Obed,' he says, 'you're a good feller. Don't you give me away, now, or I'll lose my berth. The man that owns that yacht's named Davidson, and he's got a summer place right in this town.'

"'Davidson!' says I. '*Davidson?* Not young Allie Davidson?'

"'That's him,' says he. 'And he's the blankety blankest meanest low-down cub on earth. There! I feel some better. Give me another drink to take the taste of him out of my mouth.'

"'But young Davidson's gone to Boston,' I says. 'Went this morning.'

"'That be hanged!' says Ben. 'All I know is that I got a despatch from him at Newport on Monday afternoon, telling me to have the yacht abreast this town at twelve o'clock to-night, 'cause he was coming off to her then in his launch with a friend. Friend!' And he laughed and winked his starboard eye.

"I didn't say much, being too busy thinking, but Ben went on telling about other cruises with 'friends.' Oh, a steam-yacht can be a first-class imitation of hell if the right imp owns her.

Henry got speaking of one time down along the Maine coast.

"'But,' says I, referring to what he was telling, 'if she was such a nice girl and come from such nice folks, how——'

"'How do I know?' says he. 'Promises to marry and such kind of lies, I s'pose. And the plain fact is that he's really engaged to marry a swell girl in Newport.'

"He told me her name and a lot more about her. I tried to remember the most of it, but my head was whirling—and not from cherry rum, either. All I could think was: 'Obed, it's up to you! You've got to do something.'

"I was mighty glad when the sailors hailed from the shore and Ben had to go. He 'most cried when he said good-by, and went away stepping high and bringing his heels down hard. I watched the dingey row off—the tide was out. so there was barely water for her to get clear— and then I went back home to think. And I thought all the afternoon.

"Two and two made four, anyway I could add it up, but 'twas all suspicion and no real proof, that was the dickens of it. I couldn't speak to Phœbe Ann; she wouldn't b'lieve me if I did. I couldn't telegraph Cap'n Eben at Provincetown to come home that night; I'd have to tell him the whole thing and I knew his temper, so, for Barbara's sake, 'twouldn't do. I couldn't be at the shore to stop the launch leaving. What right had I to stop another man's launch, even——

"No, 'twas up to me, and I thought and thought till after supper-time. And then I had a plan— a risky chance, but *a* chance, just the same. I went up to the store and bought four feet of medium-size rubber hose and some rubber tape, same as they sell to bicycle fellers in the summer. 'Twas almost dark when I got back in sight of my shanty, and instead of going to it I jumped that board fence that me and Prince had negotiated for, hustled along the path past the notice boards ,and went down the bluff on t'other side of Davidson's p'int. And there in the deep hole by the end of the little pier, out of sight of the house on shore, was Allie's launch. By what little light there was left I could see the brass rails shining.

"But I didn't stop to admire 'em. I give one look around. Nobody was in sight. Then I ran down the pier and jumped aboard. Almost the first thing I put my hand on was what I was looking for—the bilge-pump. 'Twas a small affair, that you could lug around in one hand, but mighty handy for keeping a boat of that kind dry.

"I fitted one end of my hose to the lower end of that pump and wrapped rubber tape around the j'int till she sucked when I tried her over the side. Then I turned on the cocks in the gasoline pipes fore and aft, and noticed that the carbureter feed cup was chock full. Then I was ready for business.

"I went for'ard, climbing over the little low cabin that was just big enough for a man to crawl into, till I reached the brass cap in the deck over the gasoline-tank. Then I unscrewed the cap, run my hose down into the tank, and commenced to pump good fourteen-cents-a-gallon gasoline overboard to beat the cars. 'Twas a thirty-gallon tank, and full up. I begun to think I'd never get her empty, but I did, finally. I pumped her dry. Then I screwed the cap on again and went home, taking Allie's bilge-pump with me, for I couldn't stop to unship the hose. The tide was coming in fast.

"At nine o'clock that night I was in my skiff, rowing off to where my power-boat laid in deep water back of the bar. When I reached her I made the skiff fast astern, lit a lantern, which I put in a locker under a thwart, and set still in the pitch-dark, smoking and waiting.

"'Twas a long, wearisome wait. There was a no'thwest wind coming up, and the waves were running pretty choppy on the bar. All I could think of was that gasoline. Was there enough in the pipes and the feed cup on that launch to carry her out to where I was? Or was there too much, and would she make the yacht, after all?

"It got to be eleven o'clock. Tide was full at twelve. I was a pretty good candidate for the crazy house by this time. I'd listened till my ear-drums felt slack, like they needed reefing. And then at last I heard her coming—*chuff*-chuff! *chuff*-chuff! *chuff*-chuff!

"And *how* she did come! She walked up abreast of me, went past me, a hundred yards or so off. Thinks I: 'It's all up. He's going to make it.'

"And then, all at once, the 'chuff-chuff-ing' stopped. Started up and stopped again. I gave a hurrah, in my mind, pulled the skiff up alongside and jumped into her, taking the lantern with me, under my coat. Then I set the light between my feet, picked up the oars and started rowing.

"I rowed quiet as I could, but he heard me 'fore I got to him. I heard a scrambling noise off ahead, and then a shaky voice hollers: 'Hello! who's that?'

"'It's me,' says I, rowing harder'n ever. 'Who are you? What's the row?'

"There was more scrambling and a slam, like

a door shutting. In another two minutes I was alongside the launch and held up my lantern. Allie was there, fussing with his engine. And he was all alone.

"Alone he was, I say, fur's a body could see, but he was mighty shaky and frightened. Also, 'side of him, on the cushions, was a girl's jacket, and I thought I'd seen that jacket afore.

"'Hello!' says I. 'Is that you, Mr. Davidson? Thought you'd gone to Boston?'

"'Changed my mind,' he says. 'Got any gasoline?'

"'What you doing off here this time of night?' I says.

"'Going out to my——' He stopped. I s'pose the truth choked him. 'I was going to Provincetown,' he went on. 'Got any gasoline?'

"'What in the nation you starting to Provincetown in the middle of the night for?' I asks, innocent as could be.

"'Oh, thunder! I had business there, that's all. *Got any gasoline?*'

"I made my skiff's painter fast to a cleat on the launch and climbed aboard. 'Gasoline?' says I. 'Gasoline? Why, yes; I've got some gasoline over on my power-boat out yonder. Has yours give out? I should think you'd filled your tank 'fore you left home on such a trip as Province-

town. Maybe the pipe's plugged or something.
Have you looked ? ' And I caught hold of the
handle of the cabin-door.

"He jumped and grabbed me by the arm.
''Tain't plugged,' he yells, sharp. 'The tank's
empty, I tell you.'

"He kept pulling me away from the cabin, but
I hung onto the handle.

"'You can't be too sure,' I says. 'This door's
locked. Give me the key.'

"'I—I left the key at home,' he says. 'Don't
waste time. Go over to your boat and fetch me
some gasoline. I'll pay you well for it.'

"Then I was sartin of what I suspicioned. The
cabin was locked, but not with the key. *That*
was in the keyhole. The door was bolted *on the
inside*.

"'All right,' says I. 'I'll sell you the gasoline,
but you'll have to go with me in the skiff to get it.
Get your anchor over or this craft'll drift to
Eastham. Hurry up.'

"He didn't like the idee of leaving the launch,
but I wouldn't hear of anything else. While he
was heaving the anchor I commenced to talk to
him.

"'I didn't know but what you'd started for
foreign parts to meet that Newport girl you're
going to marry,' I says, and I spoke good and loud.

"He jumped so I thought he'd fall overboard.

"'What's that?' he shouts.

"'Why, that girl you're engaged to,' says I. 'Miss——' and I yelled her name, and how she'd gone abroad with his folks, and all.

"'Shut up!' he whispers, waving his hands, frantic. "Don't stop to lie. Hurry up!'

"''Tain't a lie. Oh, I know about it!' I hollers, as if he was deef. I meant to be heard—by him and anybody else that might be interested. I give a whole lot more partic'lars, too. He fairly shoved me into the skiff, after a spell.

" 'Now,' he says, so mad he could hardly speak, 'stop your lying and row, will you!'

"I was willing to row then. I cal'lated I'd done some missionary work by this time. Allie's guns was spiked, if I knew Barbara Saunders. I p'inted the skiff the way she'd ought to go and laid to the oars.

"My plan had been to get him aboard the skiff and row somewheres—ashore, if I could. But 'twas otherwise laid out for me. The wind was blowing pretty fresh, and the skiff was down by the stern, so's the waves kept knocking her nose round. 'Twas dark'n a pocket, too. I couldn't tell where I *was* going.

"Allie got more fidgety every minute. 'Ain't

we 'most there?' he asks. And then he gives a
screech. 'What's that ahead?'

"I turned to see, and as I done it the skiff's bow
slid up on something. I give an awful yank at
the port oar; she slewed and tilted; a wave
caught her underneath, and the next thing I knew
me and Allie and the skiff was under water,
bound for the bottom. We'd run acrost one of
the guy-ropes of my fish-weir.

"This wa'n't in the program. I hit sand with
a bump and pawed up for air. When I got my
head out I see a water-wheel doing business close
along-side of me. It was Allie.

"'Help!' he howls. 'Help! I'm drowning!'

"I got him by the collar, took one stroke and
bumped against the weir-nets. You know what
a fish-weir's like, don't you, Mr. Brown?—a kind
of pound, made of nets hung on ropes between
poles.

"'Help!' yells Allie, clawing the nets. 'I
can't swim in rough water!'

"You might have known he couldn't. It
looked sort of dubious for a jiffy. Then I had
an idee. I dragged him to the nighest weir-pole.
'Climb!' I hollers in his ear. 'Climb that pole.'

"He done it, somehow, digging his toes into
the net and going up like a cat up a tree. When
he got to the top he hung acrost the rope and shook.

"'Hang on there!' says I. 'I'm going after the boat.' And I struck out. He yelled to me not to leave him, but the weir had give me my bearings, and I was bound for my power-boat. 'Twas a tough swim, but I made it, and climbed aboard, not feeling any too happy. Losing a good skiff was more'n I'd figgered on.

"Soon's I got some breath I hauled anchor, started up my engine and headed back for the weir. I run along-side of it, keeping a good lookout for guy-ropes, and when I got abreast of that particular pole I looked for Allie. He was setting on the rope, a-straddle of the pole, and hanging onto the top of it like it owed him money. He looked a good deal more comfortable than I was when he and Prince had treed me. And the remembrance of that time come back to me, and one of them things they call inspiration come with it. He was four feet above water, 'twas full tide then, and if he set still he was safe as a church.

"So instead of running in after him, I slowed 'way down and backed off.

"'Come here!' he yells. 'Come here, you fool, and take me aboard.'

"'Oh, I don't know,' says I. 'You're safe there, and, even if the yacht folks don't come hunting for you by and by—which I cal'late they will— the tide'll be low enough in five hours or so, so's you can walk ashore.'

"'What—what do you mean?' he says. 'Ain't you goin' to take me off?'

"'I was,' says I, 'but I've changed my plans. And, Mr. Allie Vander-what's-your-name Davidson, there's other things—low-down, mean things —planned for this night that ain't going to come off, either. Understand that, do you?'

"He understood, I guess. He didn't answer at all. Only gurgled, like he'd swallered something the wrong way.

"Then the beautiful tit for tat of the whole business come to me, and I couldn't help rubbing it in a little. 'As a sartin acquaintance of mine once said to me,' I says, 'you look a good deal handsomer up there than you do in a boat.'

"'You—you—etcetery and so forth, continued in our next!' says he, or words to that effect.

"'That's all right,' says I, putting on the power. 'You've got no kick coming. I allow you to— er—ornament my weir-pole, and 'tain't every dude I'd let do that.'

"And I went away and, as the Fifth Reader used to say, 'let him alone in his glory.'

"I went back to the launch, pulled up her anchor and took her in tow. I towed her in to her pier, made her fast and then left her for a while. When I come back the little cabin-door was open and the girl's jacket was gone.

"Then I walked up the path to the Saunders house and it done me good to see a light in Barbara's window. I set on the steps of that house until morning keeping watch. And in the morning the yacht was gone and the weir-pole was vacant, and Cap'n Eben Saunders come on the first train.

"So's that's all there is of it. Allie hasn't come back to Bayport sence, and the last I heard he'd married that Newport girl; she has my sympathy, if that's any comfort to her.

"And Barbara? Well, for a long time she'd turn white every time I met her. But, of course, I kept my mouth shut, and she went to sea next v'yage with her dad. And now I hear she's engaged to a nice feller up to Boston.

"Oh, yes—one thing more. When I got back to my shanty that morning I wiped the chalk-mark off the door. I kind of figgered that I'd paid that debt, with back interest added."

THE LOVE OF LOBELIA 'ANKINS

THE LOVE OF LOBELIA 'ANKINS

Obed's yarn being done, and friend Davidson done too, and brown at that, Peter T. passed around another relay of cigars and we lit up. 'Twas Cap'n Eri that spoke first.

"Love's a queer disease, anyway," says he. "Ain't it, now? 'Twould puzzle you and me to figger out what that Saunders girl see to like in the Davidson critter. It must be a dreadful responsible thing to be so fascinating. I never felt that responsibleness but once—except when I got married, of course—and that was a good many years ago, when I was going to sea on long v'yages, and was cruising around the East Indies, in the latitude of our new troubles, the Philippines.

"I put in about three months on one of them little coral islands off that way once. Hottest corner in the Lord's creation, I cal'late, and the laziest and sleepiest hole ever I struck. All a feller feels like doing in them islands is just to lay on his back under a palm tree all day and eat custard-apples, and such truck.

155

"Way I come to be there was like this: I was fo'mast hand on a Boston hooker bound to Singapore after rice. The skipper's name was Perkins, Malachi C. Perkins, and he was the meanest man that ever wore a sou'-wester. I've had the pleasure of telling him so sence—'twas in Surinam 'long in '72. Well, anyhow, Perkins fed us on spiled salt junk and wormy hard-tack all the way out, and if a feller dast to hint that the same wa'n't precisely what you'd call Parker House fare, why the skipper would knock him down with a marline-spike and the first mate would kick him up and down the deck. 'Twan't a pretty performance to look at, but it beat the world for taking the craving for fancy cooking out of a man.

"Well, when I got to Singapore I was nothing but skin and bone, and considerable of the skin had been knocked off by the marline-spike and the mate's boots. I'd shipped for the v'yage out and back, but the first night in port I slipped over the side, swum ashore, and never set eyes on old Perkins again till that time in Surinam, years afterward.

"I knocked round them Singapore docks for much as a month, hoping to get a berth on some other ship, but 'twan't no go. I fell in with a Britisher named Hammond, 'Ammond, he called it, and as he was on the same hunt that I was, we kept each other comp'ny. We done odd jobs now 'n' again, and slept in sailors' lodging houses when we had the price, and under bridges or on hemp bales when we hadn't. I was too proud to write home for money, and Hammond didn't have no home to write to, I cal'late.

"But luck 'll turn if you give it time enough. One night Hammond come hurrying round to my sleeping-room—that is to say, my hemp bale —and gives me a shake, and says he:

"'Turn out, you mud 'ead, I've got you a berth.'

"'Aw, go west!' says I, and turned over to go to sleep again. But he pulled me off the bale by the leg, and that woke me up so I sensed what he was saying. Seems he'd found a feller that wanted to ship a couple of fo'mast hands on a little trading schooner for a trip over to the Java Sea.

"Well, to make a long story short, we shipped with this feller, whose name was Lazarus. I cal'late if the Lazarus in Scriptur' had been up to as many tricks and had come as nigh being a thief as our Lazarus was, he wouldn't have been so poor. Ourn was a shrewd rascal and nothing more nor less than a pearl poacher. He didn't tell us that till after we sot sail, but we was so desperate I don't know as 'twould have made much diff'rence if he had.

"We cruised round for a spell, sort of prospecting, and then we landed at a little one-horse coral island, where there wa'n't no inhabitants, but where we was pretty dead sartin there was pearl oyster banks in the lagoon. There was five of us on the schooner, a Dutchman named Rhinelander, a Coolie cook and Lazarus and Hammond and me. We put up a slab shanty on shore and went to work pearl fishing, keeping one eye out for Dutch gunboats, and always having a sago palm ready to split open so's, if we got caught, we could say we was after sago.

"Well, we done fairly good at the pearl fishing; got together quite a likely mess of pearls, and, as 'twas part of the agreement that the crew had a certain share in the stake, why, Hammond and me was figgering that we was going to make enough to more'n pay us for our long spell of starving at Singapore. Lazaras was feeling purty middling chipper, the cook was feeding us high, and everything looked lovely.

"Rhinelander and the Coolie and the skipper used to sleep aboard the boat, but Hammond and me liked to sleep ashore in the shanty. For one thing, the bunks on the schooner wa'n't none too clean, and the Coolie snored so that he'd shake the whole cabin, and start me dreaming about cyclones, and cannons firing, and lions roaring, and all kind of foolishness. I always did hate a snorer.

"One morning me and Hammond come out of the shanty, and, lo and behold you! there wa'n't no schooner to be seen. That everlasting Lazarus had put up a job on us, and had sneaked off in the night with the cook and the Dutchman, and took our share of the pearls with him. I s'pose he'd cal'lated to do it from the very first. Anyway, there we was, marooned on that little two-for-a-cent island.

"The first day we didn't do much but cuss Lazarus up hill and down dale. Hammond was the best at that kind of business ever I see. He invented more'n four hundred new kind of names for the gang on the schooner, and every one of 'em was brimstone-blue. We had fish lines in the shanty, and there was plenty of water on the island, so we knew we wouldn't starve to death nor die of thirst, anyhow.

"I've mentioned that 'twas hot in them parts? Well, that island was the hottest of 'em all. Whew! Don't talk! And, more'n that, the weather was the kind that makes you feel it's a barrel of work to live. First day we fished and slept. Next day we fished less and slept more. Third day 'twas too everlasting hot even to sleep, so we set round in the shade and fought flies and jawed each other. Main trouble was who was goin' to git the meals. Land, how we did miss that Coolie cook!

"'W'y don't yer get to work and cook something fit to heat?' says Hammond. "Ere I broke my bloomin' back 'auling in the fish, and you doing nothing but 'anging around and letting 'em dry hup in the 'eat. Get to work and cook. Blimed if I ain't sick of these 'ere custard apples!'

"'Go and cook yourself,' says I. 'I didn't sign articles to be cook for no Johnny Bull!'

"Well, we jawed back and forth for an hour, maybe more. Two or three times we got up to have it out, but 'twas too hot to fight, so we set down again. Fin'lly we eat some supper, custard apples and water, and turned in.

"But 'twas too hot to sleep much, and I got up about three o'clock in the morning and went out and set down on the beach in the moonlight. Pretty soon out comes Hammond and sets down alongside and begins to give the weather a general overhauling, callin' it everything he could lay tongue to. Pretty soon he breaks off in the the middle of a nine-j'inted swear word and sings out:

"'Am I goin' crazy, or is that a schooner?'

"I looked out into the moonlight, and there, sure enough, was a schooner, about a mile off the island, and coming dead on. First-off we thought 'twas Lazarus coming back, but pretty soon we see 'twas a considerable smaller boat than his.

"We forgot all about how hot it was and hustled out on the reef right at the mouth of the lagoon. I had a coat on a stick, and I waved it for a signal, and Hammond set to work building a bonfire. He got a noble one blazing and then him and me stood and watched the schooner.

"She was acting dreadful queer. First she'd go ahead on one tack and then give a heave over and come about with a bang, sails flapping and everything of a shake; then she'd give another slat and go off another way; but mainly she kept right on toward the island.

"'W'at's the matter aboard there?' says Hammond. 'Is hall 'ands drunk?'

"'She's abandoned,' says I. 'That's what's the matter. There ain't *nobody* aboard of her.'

"Then we both says, 'Salvage!' and shook hands.

"The schooner came nearer and nearer. It begun to look as if she'd smash against the rocks in front of us, but she didn't. When she got opposite the mouth of the lagoon she heeled over on a new tack and sailed in between the rocks as pretty as anything ever you see. Then she run aground on the beach just about a quarter of a mile from the shanty.

"'Twas early morning when we climbed aboard of her. I thought Lazarus' schooner was dirty, but this one was nothing *but* dirt. Dirty sails, all patches, dirty deck, dirty everything.

"'Won't get much salvage on this bally tub,' says Hammond; 'she's one of them nigger fish boats, that's w'at she is.'

"I was kind of skittish about going below, 'fraid there might be some dead folks, but Hammond went. In a minute or so up he comes, looking scary.

"'There's something mighty queer down there,' says he: 'kind of w'eezing like a puffing pig.'

"'Wheezing your grandmother!' says I, but I went and listened at the hatch. 'Twas a funny noise I heard, but I knew what it was in a minute; I'd heard too much of it lately to forget it, right away.

"'It's snoring,' says I; 'somebody snoring.'

"''Eavens!' says Hammond, 'you don't s'pose it's that 'ere Coolie come back?'

"'No, no!' says I. 'Where's your common sense? The cook snored bass; this critter's snoring suppraner, and mighty poor suppraner at that.'

"'Well,' says he, ''ere goes to wake 'im hup!' And he commenced to holler, 'Ahoy!' and 'Belay, there!' down the hatch.

"First thing we heard was a kind of thump like somebody jumping out er bed. Then footsteps, running like; then up the hatchway comes a sight I shan't forget if I live to be a hundred.

"''Twas a woman, middling old, with a yeller face all wrinkles, and a chin and nose like Punch. She was dressed in a gaudy old calico gown, and had earrings in her ears. She give one look round at the schooner and the island. Then she see us and let out a whoop like a steam whistle.

"'Mulligatawny Sacremento merlasess!' she yells. 'Course that wa'n't what she said, but that's what it sounded like. Then, 'fore Hammond could stop her, she run for him and give him a rousing big hug. He was the most surprised man ever you see, stood there like a wooden image. I commenced to laff, but the next minute the woman come for me and hugged me, too.

"''Fectionate old gal,' says Hammond, grinning.

"The critter in the calirco gown was going through the craziest pantomime ever was; p'intin' off to sea and then down to deck and then up to the sails. I didn't catch on for a minute, but Hammond did. Says he:

"'Showing us w'ere this 'ere palatial yacht

come from. 'Ad a rough passage, it looks like!'

"Then the old gal commenced to get excited. She p'inted over the side and made motions like rowing. Then she p'inted down the hatch and shut her eyes and purtended to snore. After that she rowed again, all the time getting madder and madder, with her little black eyes a-snapping like fire coals and stomping her feet and shaking her fists. Fin'lly she finished up with a regular howl, you might say, of rage.

"'The crew took to the boat and left 'er asleep below,' says Hammond. ''Oly scissors: they're in for a lively time if old Nutcrackers 'ere ever catches 'em, 'ey?'

"Well, we went over the schooner and examined everything, but there wa'n't nothing of any value nowheres. 'Twas a reg'lar nigger fishing boat, with dirt and cockroaches by the pailful. At last we went ashore agin and up to the shanty, taking the old woman with us. After eating some more of them tiresome custard apples for breakfast, Hammond and me went down to look over the schooner agin. We found she'd started a plank running aground on the beach, and that 'twould take us a week to get her afloat and watertight.

"While we was doing this the woman come down and went aboard. Pretty soon we see

her going back to the shanty with her arms full
of bundles and truck. We didn't think anything of it then, but when we got home at noon,
there was the best dinner ever you see all ready
for us. Fried fish, and some kind of beans
cooked up with peppers, and tea—real store
tea—and a lot more things. Land, how we did
eat! We kept smacking our lips and rubbing
our vests to show we was enjoying everything,
and the old gal kept bobbing her head and grinning like one of them dummies you wind up
with a key.

"'Well,' says Hammond, 'we've got a cook at
last. Ain't we, old—old—— Blimed if we've
got a name for 'er yet! Here!' says he, pointing
to me. 'Looky here, missis! 'Edge! 'Edge!
that's 'im! 'Ammond! 'Ammond! that's me.
me. Now, 'oo are *you?* '

"She rattled off a name that had more double
j'ints in it than an eel.

"'Lordy!' says I; 'we never can larn that
rigamarole. I tell you! She looks for all the
world like old A'nt Lobelia Fosdick at home
down on Cape Cod. Let's call her that.'

"'She looks to me like the mother of a oyster-
man I used to know in Liverpool. 'Is name was
'Ankins. Let's split the difference and call 'er
Lobelia 'Ankins.'

"So we done it.

"Well, Hammond and me pounded and patched away at the schooner for the next three or four days, taking plenty of time off to sleep in, 'count of the heat, but getting along fairly well.

"Lobelia 'Ankins cooked and washed dishes for us. She done some noble cooking, 'specially as we wa'n't partic'lar, but we could see she had a temper to beat the Old Scratch. If anything got burned, or if the kittle upset, she'd howl and stomp and scatter things worse than a cyclone.

"I reckon 'twas about the third day that I noticed she was getting sweet on Hammond. She was giving him the best of all the vittles, and used to set at the table and look at him, softer'n and sweeter'n a bucket of molasses. Used to walk 'longside of him, too, and look up in his face and smile. I could see that he noticed it and that it was worrying him a heap. One day he says to me:

"''Edge,' says he, 'I b'lieve that 'ere chromo of a Lobelia 'Ankins is getting soft on me.'

"''Course she is,' says I; 'I see that a long spell ago.'

"'But what'll I do?' says he. 'A woman like 'er is a desp'rate character. If we hever git hashore she might be for lugging me to the church and marrying me by main force.'

"'Then you'll have to marry her, for all I see,' says I. 'You shouldn't be so fascinating.'

"That made him mad and he went off jawing to himself.

"The next day we got the schooner patched up and off the shoal and .'longside Lazarus' old landing wharf by the shanty. There was a little more tinkering to be done 'fore she was ready for sea, and we cal'lated to do it that afternoon.

"After dinner Hammond went down to the spring after some water and Lobelia 'Ankins went along with him. I laid down in the shade for a snooze, but I hadn't much more than settled myself comfortably when I heard a yell and somebody running. I jumped up just in time to see Hammond come busting through the bushes, lickety smash, with Lobelia after him, yelling like an Injun. Hammond wa'n't yelling; he was saving his breath for running.

"They wa'n't in sight more'n a minute, but went smashing and crashing through the woods into the distance. 'Twas too hot to run after 'em, so I waited a spell and then loafed off in a roundabout direction toward where I see 'em go. After I'd walked pretty nigh a mile I heard Hammond whistle. I looked, but didn't see him nowheres. Then he whistled again, and I see his head sticking out of the top of a palm tree.

"'Is she gone?' says he.

"'Yes, long ago,' says I. 'Come down.'

"It took some coaxing to git him down, but he come after a spell, and he was the scaredest man ever I see. I asked him what the matter was.

"''Edge,' says he, 'I'm a lost man. That 'ere 'orrible 'Ankins houtrage is either going to marry me or kill me. 'Edge,' he says, awful solemn, 'she tried to kiss me! S'elp me, she did!'

"Well, I set back and laughed. 'Is that why you run away?' I says.

"'No,' says he. 'When I wouldn't let 'er she hups with a rock as big as my 'ead and goes for me. There was murder in 'er eyes, 'Edge; I see it.'

"Then I laughed more than ever and told him to come back to the shanty, but he wouldn't. He swore he'd never come back again while Lobelia 'Ankins was there.

"''That's it,' says he, 'larf at a feller critter's sufferings. I honly wish she'd try to kiss you once, that's all!'

"Well, I couldn't make him budge, so I decided to go back and get the lay of the land. Lobelia was busy inside the shanty when I got there and looking black as a thundercloud, so I judged 'twa'n't best to say nothing to her, and I went down and finished the job on the schooner. At night, when I come in to supper, she met me at the door. She had a big stick in her hand and looked savage. I was a little nervous.

"'Now, Lobelia 'Ankins,' says I, 'put down that and be sociable, there's a good girl.'

"'Course I knew she couldn't understand me, but I was whistling to keep my courage up, as the saying is.

"''Ammond!' says she, p'inting toward the woods.

"''Yes,' says I, 'Hammond's taking a walk for his health.'

"''Ammond!' says she, louder, and shaking the stick.

"'Now, Lobelia,' says I, smiling smooth as butter, 'do put down that club!'

"''*Ammond!*' she fairly hollers. Then she went through the most blood-curdling panto-mime ever was, I reckon. First she comes up to me and taps me on the chest and says, ''Edge.' Then she goes creeping round the room on tip-toe, p'inting out of the winder all the time as much as to say she was pertending to walk through the woods. Then she p'ints to one of the stumps we used for chairs and screeches ''*Ammond!*' and fetches the stump an awful bang with the club. Then she comes over to me and kinder snuggles up and smiles, and says, ''Edge,' and tried to put the club in my hand.

"My topnot riz up on my head. 'Good Lord!' thinks I, 'she's making love to me so's to get me to take that club and go and thump Hammond with it!'

"I Put for the Woods."

"I was scared stiff, but Lobelia was between me and the door, so I kept smiling and backing away.

"'Now, Lobelia,' says I, 'don't be——'

"''Ammond!' says she.

"'Now, Miss 'Ankins, d-o-n't be hasty, I——'

"'*Ammond!*'

"Well, I backed faster and faster, and she follered me right up till at last I begun to run. Round and round the place we went, me scart for my life and she fairly frothing with rage. Finally I bust through the door and put for the woods at a rate that beat Hammond's going all holler. I never stopped till I got close to the palm tree. Then I whistled and Hammond answered.

"When I told him about the rumpus, he set and laughed like an idiot.

"'Ow d'you like Miss 'Ankin's love-making?' he says.

"'You'll like it less'n I do,' I says, 'if she gets up here with that club!'

"That kind of sobered him down again, and we got to planning. After a spell, we decided that our only chance was to sneak down to the schooner in the dark and put to sea, leaving Lobelia alone in her glory.

"Well, we waited till twelve o'clock or so and then we crept down to the beach, tiptoeing past the shanty for fear of waking Lobelia. We got on the schooner all right, hauled up anchor, h'isted sail and stood out of the lagoon with a fair wind. When we was fairly to sea we shook hands.

"'Lawd!' says Hammond, drawing a long breath, 'I never was so 'appy in my life. This 'ere lady-killing business ain't in my line. '

"He felt so good that he set by the wheel and sung, 'Good-by, sweet'art, good-by,' for an hour or more.

"In the morning we was in sight of another small island, and, out on a p'int, was a passel of folks jumping up and down and waving a signal.

"'Well, if there ain't more castaways!' says I.

"'Don't go near 'em!' says Hammond. 'Might come there was more Lobelias among 'em.'

"But pretty quick we see the crowd all pile into a boat and come rowing off to us. They was all men, and their signal was a red flannel shirt on a pole.

"We put about for 'em and picked 'em up, letting their boat tow behind the schooner. There was five of 'em, a ragged and dirty lot of Malays and half-breeds. When they first climbed aboard, I see 'em looking the schooner over mighty sharp, and in a minute they was all jabbering together in native lingo.

"'What's the matter with 'em?' says Hammond.

"A chap with scraggy black whiskers and a sort of worried look on his face, stepped for'ard and made a bow. He looked like a cross be-

tween a Spaniard and a Malay, and I guess that's
what he was.

"'Senors,' says he, palavering and scraping,
'boat! my boat!'

"'W'at's 'e giving us?' says Hammond.

"'Boat! This boat! My boat, senors,' says
the feller. All to once I understood him.

"'Hammond,' I says, 'I swan to man if I don't
believe we've picked up the real crew of this
craft!'

"'Si, senor; boat, my boat! Crew! Crew!'
says Whiskers, waving his hands toward the
rest of his gang.

"'Hall right, skipper,' says Hammond; 'glad
to see yer back haboard. Make yerselves well
at 'ome. 'Ow d' yer lose er in the first place?'

"The feller didn't seem to understand much
of this, but he looked more worried than ever.
The crew looked frightened, and jabbered.

"'Ooman, senors,' says Whiskers, in half a
whisper. 'Ooman, she here?'

"'Hammond,' says I, 'what's a ooman?'
The feller seemed to be thinkin' a minute; then
he began to make signs. He pulled his nose
down till it most touched his chin. Then he
put his hands to his ears and made loops of his
fingers to show earrings Then he took off his
coat and wrapped it round his knees like make-

b'lieve skirts. Hammond and me looked at each other.

"'Edge,' says Hammond, ''e wants to know w'at's become of Lobelia 'Ankins.'

"'No, senor,' says I to the feller; 'ooman no here. Ooman there!' And I p'inted in the direction of our island.

"Well, sir, you oughter have seen that Malay gang's faces light up! They all bust out a grinning and laffing, and Whiskers fairly hugged me and then Hammond. Then he made one of the Malays take the wheel instead of me, and sent another one into the fo'castle after something.

"But I was curious, and I says, p'inting toward Lobelia's island:

"'Ooman your wife?'

"'No, no, no,' says he, shaking his head like it would come off, 'ooman no wife. Wife there,' and he p'inted about directly opposite from my way. 'Ooman,' he goes on, 'she no wife, she——'

"Just here the Malay come up from the fo'castle, grinning like a chessy cat and hugging a fat jug of this here palm wine that natives make. I don't know where he got it from—I thought Hammond and me had rummaged that fo'castle pretty well—but, anyhow, there it was.

"Whiskers passed the jug to me and I handed

it over to Hammond. He stood up to make a speech.

"'Feller citizens,' says he, 'I rise to drink a toast. 'Ere's to the beautchous Lobelia 'Ankins, and may she long hornament the lovely island where she now——'

"The Malay at the wheel behind us gave an awful screech. We all turned sudden, and there, standing on the companion ladder, with her head and shoulders out of the hatch, was Lobelia 'Ankins, as large as life and twice as natural.

"Hammond dropped the jug and it smashed into flinders. We all stood stock-still for a minute, like folks in a tableau. The half-breed skipper stood next to me, and I snum if you couldn't see him shrivel up like one of them things they call a sensitive plant.

"The tableau lasted while a feller might count five; then things happened. Hammond and me dodged around the deckhouse; the Malays broke and run, one up the main rigging, two down the fo'castle hatch and one out on the jib-boom. But the poor skipper wa'n't satisfied with any of them places; he started for the lee rail, and Lobelia 'Ankins started after him.

"She caught him as he was going to jump overboard and yanked him back like he was a bag of meal. She shook him, she boxed his ears, she pulled his hair, and all the time he was begging and pleading and she was screeching and jabbering at the top of her lungs. Hammond pulled me by the sleeve.

"'It'll be our turn next,' says he; 'get into the boat! Quick!'

"The little boat that the crew had come in was towing behind the schooner. We slid over the stern and dropped into it. Hammond cut the towline and we laid to the oars. Long as we was in the hearing of the schooner the powwow and rumpus kept up, but just as we was landing on the little island that the Malays had left, she come about on the port tack and stood off to sea.

"'Lobelia's running things again,' says Hammond.

"Three days after this we was took off by a Dutch gunboat. Most of the time on the island we spent debating how Lobelia come to be on the schooner. Finally we decided that she must have gone aboard to sleep that night, suspecting that we'd try to run away in the schooner just as we had tried to. We talked about Whiskers and his crew and guessed about how they came to abandon their boat in the first place. One thing we was sartin sure of, and that was that they'd left Lobelia aboard on purpose. We knew mighty well that's what we'd a-done.

"What puzzled us most was what relation Lobelia was to the skipper. She wa'n't his wife, 'cause he'd said so, and she didn't look enough like him to be his mother or sister. But as we was being took off in the Dutchman's yawl, Hammond thumps the thwart with his fist and says he:

"'I've got it!' he says; 'she's 'is mother-in-law!'

"''Course she is!' says I. 'We might have known it!'"

THE MEANNESS OF ROSY

THE MEANNESS OF ROSY

Cap'n Jonadab said that the South Seas and them islands was full of queer happenings, anyhow. Said that Eri's yarn reminded him of one that Jule Sparrow used to tell. There was a Cockney in that yarn, too, and a South Sea woman and a schooner. But in other respects the stories was different.

"You all know Wash Sparrow, here in Wellmouth," says the Cap'n. "He's the laziest man in town. It runs in his family. His dad was just the same. The old man died of creeping paralysis, which was just the disease he'd pick out *to* die of, and even then he took six years to do it in. Washy's brother Jule, Julius Cæsar Sparrow, he was as no-account and lazy as the rest. When he was around this neighborhood he put in his time swapping sea lies for heat from the post-office stove, and the only thing that would get him livened up at all was the mention of a feller named 'Rosy' that he knew while he was seafaring, way off on t'other side of the world.

181

Jule used to say that 'twas this Rosy that made him lose faith in human nature.

"The first time ever Julius and Rosy met was one afternoon just as the *Emily*—that was the little fore-and-aft South Sea trading schooner Jule was in—was casting off from the ramshackle landing at Hello Island. Where's Hello Island? Well, I'll tell you. When you get home you take your boy's geography book and find the map of the world. About amidships of the sou'western quarter of it you'll see a place where the Pacific Ocean is all broke out with the measles. Yes; well, one of them measle spots is Hello Island.

" 'Course that ain't the real name of it. The real one is spelt with four o's, three a's, five i's, and a peck measure of h's and x's hove in to fill up. It looks like a plate of hash and that's the way it's pronounced. Maybe you might sing it if 'twas set to music, but no white man ever *said* the whole of it. Them that tried always broke down on the second fathom or so and said 'Oh, the hereafter!' or words to that effect. 'Course the missionaries see that wouldn't do, so they twisted it stern first and it's been Hello Island to most folks ever since.

"Why Jule was at Hello Island is too long a yarn. Biled down it amounts to a voyage on a bark out of Seattle, and a first mate like yours,

Eri, who was a kind of Christian Science chap
and cured sick sailors by the laying on of hands
—likewise feet and belaying pins and ax handles
and such. And, according to Jule's tell, he *did*
cure 'em, too. After he'd jumped up and down
on your digestion a few times you forgot all about
the disease you started in with and only remembered the complications. Him and Julius had
their final argument one night when the bark
was passing abreast one of the Navigator Islands,
close in. Jule hove a marlinespike at the mate's
head and jumped overboard. He swum ashore
to the beach and, inside of a week, he'd shipped
aboard the *Emily*. And 'twas aboard the *Emily*,
and at Hello Island, as I said afore, that he met
Rosy.

"George Simmons—a cockney Britisher he
was, and skipper—was standing at the schooner's
wheel, swearing at the two Kanaka sailors who
were histing the jib. Julius, who was mate,
was roosting on the lee rail amid-ships, helping
him swear. And old Teunis Van Doozen, a
Dutchman from Java or thereabouts, who was
cook, was setting on a stool by the galley door
ready to heave in a word whenever 'twas necessary.
The Kanakas was doing the work. That was
the usual division of labor aboard the Emily.

"Well, just then there comes a yell from the

bushes along the shore. Then another yell and
a most tremendous cracking and smashing. Then
out of them bushes comes tearing a little man
with spectacles and a black enamel-cloth carpetbag, heaving sand like a steam-shovel and seemingly trying his best to fly. And astern of him
comes more yells and a big, husky Kanaka woman,
about eight foot high and three foot in the beam,
with her hands stretched out and her fingers
crooked.

"Julius used to swear that that beach was all
of twenty yards wide and that the little man only
lit three times from bush to wharf. And he
didn't stop there. He fired the carpetbag at the
schooner's stern and then spread out his wings
and flew after it. His fingers just hooked over
the rail and he managed to haul himself aboard.
Then he curled up on the deck and breathed short
but spirited. The Kanaka woman danced to
the stringpiece and whistled distress signals.

"Cap'n George Simmons looked down at the
wrecked flying machine and grunted.

"'Umph!' says he. 'You don't look like a
man the girls would run after. Lady your wife?'

"The little feller bobbed his specs up and
down.

"'So?' says George. ''Ow can I bear to
leave thee,' 'ey? Well, ain't you ashamed of

yourself to be running off and leaving a nice, 'andsome, able-bodied wife that like? Look at 'er now, over there on 'er knees a praying for you to come back.'

"There was a little p'int making out from the beach close by the edge of the channel and the woman was out on the end of it, down on all fours. Her husband raised up and looked over the rail.

"'She ain't praying,' he pants, ducking down again quick. 'She's a-picking up stones.'

"And so she was. Julius said he thought sure she'd cave in the Emily's ribs afore she got through with her broadsides. The rocks flew like hail. Everybody got their share, but Cap'n George got a big one in the middle of the back. That took his breath so all the way he could express his feelings was to reach out and give his new passenger half a dozen kicks. But just as soon as he could he spoke, all right enough.

"'You mis'rable four-eyed shrimp!' he says. ''Twould serve you right if I 'ove to and made you swim back to 'er. Blow me if I don't believe I will!'

"'Aw, don't, Cap'n; *please* don't!' begs the feller. 'I'll be awful grateful to you if you won't. And I'll make it right with you, too. I've got a good thing in that bag of mine. Yes, sir! A beautiful good thing.'

"'Oh, well,' says the skipper, bracing up and smiling sweet as he could for the ache in his back. 'I'll 'elp you out. You trust your Uncle George. Not on account of what you're going to give me, you understand,' says he. "It would be a pity if *that* was the reason for 'elpin' a feller creat— Sparrow, if you touch that bag I'll break your blooming 'ead. 'Ere! you 'and it to me. I'll take care of it for the gentleman.'

"All the rest of that day the Cap'n couldn't do enough for the passenger. Give him a big dinner that took Teunis two hours to cook, and let him use his own pet pipe with the last of Jule's tobacco in it, and all that. And that evening in the cabin, Rosy told his story. Seems he come from Bombay originally, where he was born an innocent and trained to be a photographer. This was in the days when these hand cameras wa'n't so common as they be now, and Rosy—his full name was Clarence Rosebury, and he looked it—had a fine one. Also he had some plates and photograph paper and a jug of 'developer' and bottles of stuff to make more, wrapped up in an old overcoat and packed away in the carpetbag. He had landed in the Fijis first—off and had drifted over to Hello Island, taking pictures of places and natives and so on, intending to use 'em in a course of lectures he was going to deliver when he got back home. He boarded with the Kanaka lady at Hello till his money give out, and then he married her to save board. He wouldn't talk about his married life—just shivered instead.

"'But w'at about this good thing you was mentioning, Mr. Rosebury?' asks Cap'n George, polite, but staring hard at the bag. Jule and the cook was in the cabin likewise. The skipper would have liked to keep 'em out, but they being two to one, he couldn't.

"'That's it,' answers Rosy, cheerful.

"'W'at's it?'

"'Why, the things in the grip; the photograph things. You see,' says Rosy, getting excited, his innocent, dreamy eyes a-shining behind his specs and the ridge of red hair around his bald spot waving like a hedge of sunflowers; 'you see,' he says, 'my experience has convinced me that there's a fortune right in these islands for a photographer who'll take pictures of the natives. They're all dying to have their photographs took. Why, when I was in Hello Island I could have took dozens, only they didn't have the money to pay for 'em and I couldn't wait till they got some. But you've got a schooner. You could sail around from one island to another, me taking pictures and you getting copra and—and pearls and things from the natives in trade for 'em.

And we'd leave a standing order for more plates to be delivered steady from the steamer at Suva or somewheres, and——'

"'Old on!' Cap'n George had been getting redder and redder in the face while Rosy was talking, and now he fairly biled over, like a teakettle. ''Old on!' he roars. 'Do I understand that *this* is the good thing you was going to let me in on? Me to cruise you around from Dan to Beersheby, feeding you, and giving you tobacco to smoke——'

"''Twas my tobacco,' breaks in Julius.

"'Shut up! Cruising you around, and you living on the fat of—of the—the water, and me trusting to get my pay out of tintypes of Kanakas! Was that it? Was it?'

"'Why—why, yes,' answers Rosy. 'But, cap'n, you don't understand——'

"'Then,' says George, standing up and rolling up his pajama sleeves, 'there's going to be justifiable 'omicide committed right now.'

"Jule said that if it hadn't been that the skipper's sore back got to hurting him he don't know when him and the cook would have had their turn at Rosy. 'Course they wanted a turn on account of the tobacco and the dinner, not to mention the stone bruises. When all hands was through, that photographer was a spiled negative.

"And that was only the beginning. They

ain't much fun abusing Kanakas because they
don't talk back, but first along Rosy would try
to talk back, and that give 'em a chance. Julius
had learned a lot of things from that mate on the
bark, and he tried 'em all on that tintype man.
And afterward they invented more. They made
him work his passage, and every mean and dirty
job there was to do, he had to do it. They took
his clothes away from him, and, while they lasted,
the skipper had three shirts at once, which hadn't
happened afore since he served his term in the
Sydney jail. And he was such a *comfort* to 'em.
Whenever the dinner wa'n't cooked right, instead
of blaming Teunis, they took it out of Rosy. By
the time they made their first port they wouldn't
have parted with him for no money, and they
locked him up in the fo'castle and kept him there.
And when one of the two Kanaka boys run
away they shipped Rosy in his place by unanimous vote. And so it went for six months,
the *Emily* trading and stealing all around the
South Seas.

"One day the schooner was off in an out-of-the
way part of the ocean, and the skipper come up
from down below, bringing one of the photo-
graphing bottles from the carpetbag.

"'See 'ere,' says he to Rosy, who was swabbing decks just to keep him out of mischief, 'w'at

kind of a developer stuff is this? It has a mighty familiar smell.'

"'That ain't developer, sir,' answers Rosy, meek as usual. 'That's alcohol. I use it——'

"'Alcohol!' says George. 'Do you mean to tell me that you've 'ad alcohol aboard all this time and never said a word to one of us? If that ain't just like you! Of all the ungrateful beasts as ever I——'

"When him and the other two got through convincing Rosy that he was ungrateful, they took that bottle into the cabin and begun experimenting. Julius had lived a few months in Maine, which is a prohibition State, and so he knew how to make alcohol 'splits'—one-half wet fire and the rest water. They 'split' for five days. Then the alcohol was all out and the *Emily* was all in, being stove up on a coral reef two mile off shore of a little island that nobody'd ever seen afore.

"They got into the boat—the four white men and the Kanaka—histed the sail, and headed for the beach. They landed all right and was welcomed by a reception committee of fifteen husky cannibals with spears, dressed mainly in bone necklaces and sunshine. The committee was glad to see 'em, and showed it, particular to Teunis, who was fat. Rosy, being principally framework by this time, wa'n't nigh so popular; but he didn't seem to care.

"The darkies tied 'em up good and proper and then held a committee meeting, arguing, so Julius cal'lated, whether to serve 'em plain or with greens. While the rest was making up the bill of fare, a few set to work unpacking the bags and things, Rosy's satchel among 'em. Pretty soon there was an awful jabbering.

"'They've settled it,' says George, doleful. 'Well, there's enough of Teunis to last 'em for one meal, if they ain't 'ogs. You're a tough old bird, cooky; maybe you'll give 'em dyspepsy, so they won't care for the rest of us. That's a ray of 'ope, ain't it?'

"But the cook didn't seem to get much hope out of it. He was busy telling the skipper what he thought of him when the natives come up. They was wildly excited, and two or three of 'em was waving square pieces of cardboard in their hands.

"And here's where the *Emily's* gang had a streak of luck. The Kanaka sailor couldn't talk much English, but it seems that his granddad, or some of his ancestors, must have belonged to the same breed of cats as these islanders, for he could manage to understand a little of their lingo.

"'Picture!' says he, crazy-like with joy. 'Picture, cappy; picture!'

"When Rosy was new on board the schooner, afore George and the rest had played with him till he was an old story, one of their games was to have him take their photographs. He'd taken the cap'n's picture, and Julius's and Van Doozen's. The pictures was a Rogues' Gallery that would have got 'em hung on suspicion anywhere in civilization, but these darkies wa'n't particular. Anyhow they must have been good likenesses, for the committee see the resemblance right off.

"'They t'ink witchcraft,' says the Kanaka. 'Want to know how make.'

"'Lord!' says George. 'You tell 'em we're witches from Witch Center. Tell 'em we make them kind of things with our eyes shut, and if they eat us we'll send our tintypes to 'aunt 'em into their graves. Tell 'em that quick.'

"Well, I guess the Kanaka obeyed orders, for the islanders was all shook up. They jabbered and hurrahed like a parrot-house for ten minutes or so. Then they untied the feet of their Sunday dinners, got 'em into line, and marched 'em off across country, prodding 'em with their spears, either to see which was the tenderest or to make 'em step livelier, I don't know which.

"Julius said that was the most nervous walk ever he took. Said afore 'twas done he was so leaky with spear holeˢ that he cast a shadder like a skimmer. Just afore sunset they come to the other side of the island, where there was a good sized native village, with houses made of grass and cane, and a big temple-like in the middle, decorated fancy and cheerful with skulls and spareribs. Jule said there was places where the decorations needed repairs, and he figgered he was just in time to finish 'em. But he didn't take no pride in it; none of his folks cared for art.

"The population was there to meet 'em, and even the children looked hungry. Anybody could see that having company drop in for dinner was right to their taste. There was a great chair arrangement in front of the temple, and on it was the fattest, ugliest, old liver-colored woman that Julius ever see. She was rigged up regardless, with a tooth necklace and similar jewelry; and it turned out that she was the queen of the bunch. Most of them island tribes have chiefs, but this district was strong for woman suffrage.

"Well, the visitors had made a hit, but Rosy's photographs made a bigger one. The queen and the head men of the village pawed over 'em and compared 'em with the originals and powwowed like a sewing circle. Then they called up the Kanaka sailor, and he preached witchcraft and hoodoos to beat the cars, lying as only a feller that knows the plates are warming for him on the back of the stove can lie.   Finally the queen wanted to know if the 'long pigs' could make a witch picture of *her*.

"'Tell 'er yes,' yells George, when the question was translated to him. 'Tell 'er we're picture-makers by special app'intment to the Queen and the Prince of Wales. Tell 'er we'll make 'er look like the sweetest old chocolate drop in the taffy-shop. Only be sure and say we must 'ave a day or so to work the spells and put on the kibosh.'

"So 'twas settled, and dinner was put off for that night, anyhow. And the next day being sunny, Rosy took the queen's picture. 'Twas an awful strain on the camera, but it stood it fine; and the photographs he printed up that afternoon was the most horrible collection of mince-pie dreams that ever a sane man run afoul of.   Rosy used one of the grass huts for a dark room; and while he was developing them plates, they could hear him screaming from sheer fright at being shut up alone with 'em in the dark.

"But her majesty thought they was lovely, and set and grinned proud at 'em for hours at a stretch. And the wizards was untied and fed up and given the best house in town to live in. And Cap'n George and Julius and the cook got to feeling so cheerful and happy that they begun to kick Rosy again, just out of habit. And so it went on for three days.

"Then comes the Kanaka interpreter—grinning kind of foolish.

"'Cappy,' says he, 'queen, she likes you. She likes you much lot.'

Rosy took the Queen's Picture.

"'Well,' says the skipper, modest, 'she'd ought to. She don't see a man like me every day. She ain't the first woman,' he says.

"'She like all you gentlemen,' says the Kanaka.

'She say she want witch husband. One of you got marry her.'

"'*Hey?*' yells all hands, setting up.

"'Yes, sir. She no care which one, but one white man must marry her to-morrow. Else we all go chop plenty quick.'

"'Chop' is Kanaka English for 'eat.' There wa'n't no need for the boy to explain.

"Then there was times. They come pretty nigh to a fight, because Teunis and Jule argued that the skipper, being such a ladies' man, was the natural-born choice. Just as things was the warmest, Cap'n George had an idea.

"'*Rosy!*' says he.

"'Hey ?' says the others. Then, 'Rosy ? Why, of course, Rosy's the man.'

"But Rosy wa'n't agreeable. Julius said he never see such a stubborn mule in his life. They tried every reasonable way they could to convince him, pounding him on the head and the like of that, but 'twas no go.

"'I got a wife already,' he says, whimpering. 'And, besides, cap'n, there wouldn't be such a contrast in looks between you and her as there would with me.'

"He meant so far as size went, but George took it the other way, and there was more trouble. Finally Julius come to the rescue.

"'I tell you,' says he. 'We'll be square and draw straws!'

"'W'at?' hollers George. 'Well, I guess not!'

"'And I'll hold the straws,' says Jule, winking on the side.

"So they drew straws, and, strange as it may seem, Rosy got stuck. He cried all night, and though the others tried to comfort him, telling him what a lucky man he was to marry a queen, he wouldn't cheer up a mite.

"And next day the wedding took place in the temple in front of a wood idol with three rows of teeth, and as ugly almost as the bride, which was saying a good deal. And when 'twas over, the three shipmates come and congratulated the groom, wishing him luck and a happy honeymoon and such. Oh, they had a bully time, and they was still laughing over it that night after supper, when down comes a file of big darkies with spears, the Kanaka interpreter leading 'em.

"'Cappy,' says he. 'The king say you no stay in this house no more. He say too good for you. Say, bimeby, when the place been clean up, maybe he use it himself. You got to go.'

"'Who says this?' roars Cap'n George, ugly as could be.

"'The king, he say it.'

"'The queen, you mean. There ain't no king.'

"'Yes, sir. King *and* queen now. Mr. Rosy he king. All tribe proud to have witch king.'

"The three looked at each other.

"'Do you mean to say,' says the skipper, choking so he could hardly speak, 'that we've got to take orders from '*im?*'

"'Yes, sir. King say you no mind, we make.'

"Well, sir, the language them three used must have been something awful, judging by Jule's tell. But when they vowed they wouldn't move, the spears got busy and out they had to get and into the meanest, dirtiest little hut in the village, one without hardly any sides and great holes in the roof. And there they stayed all night in a pouring rain, the kind of rains you get in them islands.

"''Twa'n't a nice night. They tried huddling together to keep dry, but 'twa'n't a success because there was always a row about who should be in the middle. Then they kept passing personal remarks to one another.

"'If the skipper hadn't been so gay and uppish about choosing Rosy,' says Julius, 'there wouldn't have been no trouble. I do hate a smart Aleck.'

"'Who said draw straws?' sputters George, mad clean through. 'And who 'eld 'em? 'Ey? Who did?'

"'Well,' says Teunis, '*I* didn't do it. You can't blame me.'

"'No. You set there like a bump on a log and let me and the mate put our feet in it. You old fat 'ead! I——'

"They pitched into the cook until he got mad and hit the skipper. Then there was a fight that lasted till they was all scratched up and tired out. The only thing they could agree on was that Rosy was what the skipper called a 'viper' that they'd nourished in their bosoms.

"Next morning 'twas worse than ever. Down comes the Kanaka with his spear gang and routs 'em out and sets 'em to gathering breadfruit all day in the hot sun. And at night 'twas back to the leaky hut again.

"And that wa'n't nothing to what come later. The lives that King Rosy led them three was something awful. 'Twas dig in and work day in and day out. Teunis had to get his majesty's meals, and nothing was ever cooked right; and then the royal army got after the steward with spear handles. Cap'n George had to clean up the palace every day, and Rosy and the queen—who was dead gone on her witch husband, and let him do anything he wanted to—stood over him and found fault and punched him with sharp sticks to see him jump. And Julius had to fetch and carry and wait, and get on his knees whenever he spoke to the king, and be helped up again with a kick, like as not.

"Rosy took back all his own clothes that they'd stole, and then he took theirs for good measure. He made 'em marry the three ugliest old women on the island—his own bride excepted—and when they undertook to use a club or anything, he had *them* licked instead. He wore 'em down to skin and bone. Jule said you wouldn't believe a mortal man could treat his feller creatures so low down and mean. And the meanest part of it was that he always called 'em the names that they used to call him aboard ship. Sometimes he invented new ones, but not often, because 'twa'n't necessary.

"For a good six months this went on—just the same length of time that Rosy was aboard the *Emily*. Then, one morning early, Julius looks out of one of the holes in the roof of his house and, off on the horizon, heading in, he sees a small steamer, a pleasure yacht 'twas. He lets out a yell that woke up the village, and races head first for the *Emily's* boat that had been rowed around from the other side of the island, and laid there with her oars and sail still in her. And behind him comes Van Doozen and Cap'n George.

"Into the boat they piled, while the islanders were getting their eyes open and gaping at the steamer. There wa'n't no time to get up sail, so they grabbed for the oars. She stuck on the sand just a minute; and, in that minute, down from the palace comes King Rosy, running the way he run from his first wife over at Hello. He leaped over the stern, picked up the other oar, and off they put across the lagoon. The rudder was in its place and so was the tiller, but they couldn't use 'em then.

"They had a good start, but afore they'd got very far the natives had waked up and were after 'em in canoes.

"'Ere!' screams Cap'n George. 'This won't do! They'll catch us sure. Get sail on to 'er lively! Somebody take that tiller.'

"Rosy, being nearest, took the tiller and the others got up the sail. Then 'twas nip and tuck with the canoes for the opening of the barrier reef at the other side of the lagoon. But they made it first, and, just as they did, out from behind the cliff comes the big steam-yacht, all white and shining, with sailors in uniform on her decks, and awnings flapping, and four mighty pretty women leaning over the side. All of the *Emily* gang set up a whoop of joy, and 'twas answered from the yacht.

"'Saved!' hollers Cap'n George. 'Saved, by thunder! And now,' says he, knocking his fists together, '*now* to get square with that four-eyed thief in the stern! Come on, boys!'

"Him and Julius and Teunis made a flying leap aft to get at Rosy. But Rosy see 'em coming, jammed the tiller over, the boom swung across and swept the the three overboard pretty as you please.

"There was a scream from the yacht. Rosy give one glance at the women. Then he tossed his arms over his head.

"'Courage, comrades!' he shouts. 'I'll save you or die with you!'

"And overboard he dives, 'kersplash!'

"Julius said him and the skipper could have swum all right if Rosy had give 'em the chance, but he didn't. He knew a trick worth two of that. He grabbed 'em round the necks and kept hauling 'em under and splashing and kicking like a water-mill. All hands was pretty well used up when they was pulled aboard the yacht.

"'Oh, you brave man!' says one of the women, stooping over Rosy, who was sprawled on the deck with his eyes shut, 'Oh, you *hero!*'

"'Are they living?' asks Rosy, faint-like and opening one eye. 'Good! Now I can die content.'

"'Living!' yells George, soon's he could get the salt water out of his mouth. 'Living! By the 'oly Peter! Let me at 'im! I'll show 'im whether I'm living or not!'

"'What ails you, you villain?' says the feller that owned the yacht, a great big Englishman, Lord Somebody-or-other. 'The man saved your lives.'

"'He knocked us overboard!' yells Julius.

"'Yes, and he done it a-purpose!' sputters Van Doozen, well as he could for being so water-logged.

"'Let's kill him!' says all three.

"'Did it on purpose!' says the lord, scornful. 'Likely he'd throw you over and then risk his life to save you. Here!' says he to the mate. 'Take those ungrateful rascals below. Give 'em dry clothes and then set 'em to work—hard work; understand? As for this poor, brave chap, take him to the cabin. I hope he'll pull through,' says he.

"And all the rest of the voyage, which was to Melbourne, Julius and his two chums had to slave and work like common sailors, while Rosy, the hero invalid, was living on beef tea and jelly and champagne, and being petted and fanned by the lord's wife and the other women. And 'twas worse toward the end, when he pretended to be

feeling better, and could set in a steamer-chair
on deck and grin and make sarcastic remarks
under his breath to George and the other two
when they was holystoning or scrubbing in the
heat.

"At Melbourne they hung around the wharf,
waiting to lick him, till the lord had 'em took up
for vagrants. When they got out of the lockup
they found Rosy had gone. And his lordship
had given him money and clothes, and I don't
know what all.

"Julius said that Rosy's meanness sickened
him of the sea. Said 'twas time to retire when
such reptiles was afloat. So he come home and
married the scrub-woman at the Bay View House.
He lived with her till she lost her job. I don't
know where he is now."

* * * * * *

'Twas purty quiet for a few minutes after
Jonadab had unloaded this yarn. Everybody
was busy trying to swaller his share of the state-
ments in it, I cal'late. Peter T. looked at the
Cap'n, admiring but reproachful.

"Wixon," says he. "I didn't know 'twas in
you. Why didn't you tell me?"

"Oh," says Jonadab, "I ain't responsible.
'Twas Jule Sparrow that told it to me."

"Humph!" says Peter. "I wish you knew his

address. I'd like to hire him to write the Old Home ads. I thought *my* invention was A 1, but I'm in the kindergarten. Well, let's go to bed before somebody tries to win the prize from Sparrow."

'Twas after eleven by then, so, as his advice looked good, we follered it.

THE ANTIQUERS

THE ANTIQUERS

We've all got a crazy streak in us somewheres, I cal'late, only the streaks don't all break out in the same place, which is a mercy, when you come to think of it. One feller starts tooting a fish horn and making announcements that he's the Angel Gabriel. Another poor sufferer shows his first symptom by having his wife's relations come and live with him. One ends in the asylum and t'other in the poorhouse; that's the main difference in them cases. Jim Jones fiddles with perpetual motion and Sam Smith develops a sure plan for busting Wall Street and getting rich sudden. I take summer boarders maybe, and you collect postage stamps. Oh, we're all looney, more or less, every one of us.

Speaking of collecting reminds me of the "Antiquers"—that's what Peter T. Brown called 'em. They put up at the Old Home House— summer before last; and at a crank show they'd have tied for the blue ribbon. There was the Dowager and the Duchess and "My Daughter" and Irene dear." Likewise there was Thompson and Small, but they, being nothing but husbands and fathers, didn't count for much first along, except when board was due or "antiques" had to be settled for.

The Dowager fetched port first. She hove alongside the Old Home one morning early in July, and she had "My Daughter" in tow. The names, as entered on the shipping list, was Mrs. Milo Patrick Thompson and Miss Barbara Millicent Thompson, but Peter T. Brown he had 'em re-entered as "The Dowager" and "My Daughter" almost as soon as they dropped anchor. Thompson himself come poking up to the dock on the following Saturday night; Peter didn't christen him, except to chuck out something about Milo's being an "also ran."

The Dowager was skipper of the Thompson craft, with "My daughter"—that's what her ma always called her—as first mate, and Milo as general roustabout and purser.

'Twould have done you good to see the fleet run into the breakfast room of a morning, with the Dowager leading, under full sail, Barbara close up to her starboard quarter, and Milo tailing out a couple of lengths astern. The other boarders looked like quahaug dories abreast of the Marblehead Yacht Club. Oh, the Thompsons won every cup until the Smalls arrived on a Monday; then 'twas a dead heat.

Mamma Small was built on the lines of old lady Thompson, only more so, and her daughter flew pretty nigh as many pennants as Barbara. Peter T. had 'em labeled the "Duchess" and "Irene dear" in a jiffy. He didn't nickname Small any more'n he had Thompson, and for the same reasons. Me and Cap'n Jonadab called Small "Eddie" behind his back, 'count of his wife's hailing him as "Edwin."

Well, the Dowager and the Duchess sized each other up, and, recognizing I jedge, that they was sister ships, set signals and agreed to cruise in company and watch out for pirates—meaning young men without money who might want to talk to their daughters. In a week the four women was thicker than hasty-pudding and had thrones on the piazza where they could patronize everybody short of the Creator, and criticize the other boarders. Milo and Eddie got friendly too, and found a harbor behind the barn where they could smoke and swap sympathy.

'Twas fair weather for pretty near a fortni't, and then she thickened up. The special brand of craziness in Wellmouth that season was collecting "antiques," the same being busted chairs and invalid bureaus and sofys that your great grandmarm got ashamed of and sent to the sick-bay a thousand year ago. Oh, yes, and dishes! If there was one thing that would drive a city woman to counting her fingers and cutting paper dolls, 'twas a nicked blue plate with a Chinese picture on it. And the homelier the plate the higher the price. Why there was as many as six families that got enough money for the rubbage in their garrets to furnish their houses all over with brand new things—real shiny, hand-painted stuff, not haircloth ruins with music box springs, nor platters that you had to put a pan under for fear of losing cargo.

I don't know who fetched the disease to the Old Home House. All I'm sartain of is that 'twan't long afore all hands was in that condition where the doctor'd have passed 'em on to the parson. First along it seemed as if the Thompson-Small syndicate had been vaccinated—they didn't develop a symptom. But one noon the Dowager sails into the dining-room and unfurls a brown paper bundle.

"I've captured a prize, my dear," says she to the Duchess. "A veritable prize. Just look!"

And she dives under the brown paper hatches and resurrects a pink plate, suffering from yaller jaundice, with the picture of a pink boy, wearing curls and a monkey-jacket, holding hands with a pink girl with pointed feet.

"Ain't it perfectly lovely?" says she, waving the outrage in front of the Duchess. "A ginuwine Hall nappy! And in *such* condition!"

"Why," says the Duchess, "I didn't know you were interested in antiques."

"I dote on 'em," comes back the Dowager, and "my daughter" owned up that she "adored" 'em.

"If you knew," continues Mrs. Thompson, "how I've planned and contrived to get this treasure. I've schemed— My! my! My daughter says she's actually ashamed of me. Oh, no! I can't tell even *you* where I got it. All's fair in love and collecting, you know, and there are more gems where this came from."

She laughed and "my daughter" laughed, and the Duchess and "Irene dear" laughed, too, and said the plate was "*so* quaint," and all that, but you could fairly hear 'em turn green with jealeusy. It didn't need a spyglass to see that they wouldn't ride easy at their own moorings till *they'd* landed a treasure or two—probably two.

And sure enough, in a couple of days they bore down on the Thompsons, all sail set and colors flying. They had a pair of plates that for ugliness and price knocked the "ginuwine Hall nappy" higher 'n the main truck. And the way they

crowed and bragged about their "finds" wa'n't fit
to put in the log. The Dowager and "my daughter" left that dinner table trembling all over.

Well, you can see how a v'yage would end that
commenced that way. The Dowager and Barbara would scour the neighborhood and capture
more prizes, and the Duchess and her tribe would
get busy and go 'em one better. That's one sure
p'int about the collecting business—it'll stir up
a fight quicker'n anything I know of, except
maybe a good looking bachelor minister. The
female Thompsons and Smalls was "my dear-in'"
each other more'n ever, but there was a chill
setting in round them piazza thrones, and some of
the sarcastic remarks that was casually hove out
by the bosom friends was pretty nigh sharp enough
to shave with. As for Milo and Eddie, they still
smoked together behind the barn, but the atmosphere on the quarter-deck was affecting the
fo'castle and there wa'n't quite so many "old
mans" and "dear boys" as there used to was.
There was a general white frost coming, and you
didn't need an Old Farmer's Almanac to prove it.

The spell of weather developed sudden. One
evening me and Cap'n Jonadab and Peter T.
was having a confab by the steps of the billiard-
room, when Milo beats up from around the corner. He was smiling as a basket of chips.

"Hello!" hails Peter T. cordial. "You look as if you'd had money left you. Any one else remembered in the will?" he says.

Milo laughed all over. "Well, well," says he, "I *am* feeling pretty good. Made a ten-strike with Mrs. T. this afternoon for sure."

"That so?" says Peter. "What's up? Hooked a prince?"

A friend of "my daughter's" over at Newport had got engaged to a mandarin or a count or something 'nother, and the Dowager had been preaching kind of eloquent concerning the shortness of the nobility crop round Wellmouth.

"No," says Milo, laughing again. "Nothing like that. But I have got hold of that antique davenport she's been dying to capture."

One of the boarders at the hotel over to Harniss had been out antiquing a week or so afore and had bagged a contraption which answered to the name of a "ginuwine Sheriton davenport." The dowager heard of it, and ever since she'd been remarking that some people had husbands who cared enough for their wives to find things that pleased 'em. She wished she was lucky enough to have that kind of a man; but no, *she* had to depend on herself, and etcetery and so forth. Maybe you've heard sermons similar.

So we was glad for Milo and said so. Likewise

we wanted to know where he found the davenport.

"Why, up here in the woods," says Milo, "at the house of a queer old stick, name of Rogers. I forget his front name—'twas longer'n the davenport."

"Not Adoniram Rogers?" says Cap'n Jonadab, wondering.

"That's him," says Thompson.

Now, I knew Adoniram Rogers. His house was old enough, Lord knows; but that a feller with a nose for a bargain like his should have hung on to a salable piece of dunnage so long as this seemed 'most too tough to believe.

"Well, I swan to man!" says I. "Adoniram Rogers! Have you seen the—the davenport thing?"

"Sure I've seen it!" says Milo. "I ain't much of a jedge, and of course I couldn't question Rogers too much for fear he'd stick on the price. But it's an old davenport, and it's got Sheriton lines and I've got the refusal of it till to-morrow, when Mrs. T's going up to inspect."

"Told Small yet?" asked Peter T., winking on the side to me and Jonadab.

Milo looked scared. "Goodness! No," says he. "And don't you tell him neither. His wife's davenport hunting too."

"You say you've got the refusal of it?" says I.

"Well, I know Adoniram Rogers, and if *I* was dickering with him I'd buy the thing first and get the refusal of it afterwards. You hear *me?*"

"Is that so?" repeats Milo. "Slippery, is he? I'll take my wife up there first thing in the morning."

He walked off looking worried, and his tops'ls hadn't much more'n sunk in the offing afore who should walk out of the billiard room behind us but Eddie Small.

"Brown," says he to Peter T., "I want you to have a horse and buggy harnessed up for me right off. Mrs. Small and I are going for a little drive to—to—over to Orham," he says.

'Twas a mean, black night for a drive as fur as Orham and Peter looked surprised. He started to say something, then swallered it down, and told Eddie he'd see to the harnessing. When Small was out of sight, I says:

"You don't cal'late he heard what Milo was telling, do you, Peter?" says I.

Peter T. shook his head and winked, first at Jonadab and then at me.

And the next day there was the dickens to pay because Eddie and the Duchess had driven up to Rogers' the night afore and had bought the davenport, refusal and all, for twenty dollars more'n Milo offered for it.

Adoniram brought it down that forenoon and all hands and the cook was on the hurricane deck to man the yards. 'Twas a wonder them boarders didn't turn out the band and fire salutes. Such ohs and ahs! 'Twan't nothing but a ratty old cripple of a sofy, with one leg carried away and most of the canvas in ribbons, but four men lugged it up the steps and the careful way they handled it made you think the Old Home House was a receiving tomb and they was laying in the dear departed.

'Twas set down on the piazza and then the friends had a chance to view the remains. The Duchess and "Irene dear" gurgled and gushed and received congratulations. Eddie stood around and tried to look modest as was possible under the circumstances. The Dowager sailed over, tilted her nose up to the foretop, remarked "Humph!" through it and come about and stood at the other end of the porch. "My daughter" follers in her wake, observes "Humph!" likewise and makes for blue water. Milo comes over and looks at Eddie.

"Well ? " says Small. "What do you think of it ? "

"Never mind what I think of *it*," answers Thompson, through his teeth. "Shall I tell *you* what I think of *you?* "

I thought for a minute that hostilities was going to begin, but they didn't. The women was the real battleships in that fleet, the men wa'n't nothing but transports. Milo and Eddie just glared at each other and sheered off, and the "ginuwine

FRIENDS HAD A CHANCE TO VIEW THE REMAINS.

Sheriton" was lugged into the sepulchre, meaning the trunk-room aloft in the hotel.

And after that the cold around the thrones was so fierce we had to move the thermometer, and we had to give the families separate tables in the dining-room so's the milk would'nt freeze. You see the pitcher set right between 'em, and— Oh! I didn't expect you'd believe it.

The "antiquing" went on harder than ever. Every time the Thompsons landed a relic, they'd bring it out on the veranda or in to dinner and gloat over it loud and pointed, while the Smalls would pipe all hands to unload sarcasm. And the same vicy vercy when 'twas t'other way about. 'Twas interesting and instructive to listen to and amused the populace on rainy days, so Peter T. said.

Adoniram Rogers had been mighty scurce 'round the Old Home sense the davenport deal. But one morning he showed up unexpected. A boarder had dug up an antique somewheres in the shape of a derelict plate, and was displaying it proud on the piazza. The Thompsons was there and the Smalls and a whole lot more. All of a sudden Rogers walks up the steps and reaches over and makes fast to the plate.

"Look out!" hollers the prize-winner, frantic. "You'll drop it!"

Adoniram grunted. "Huh!" says he. "'Tain't nothing but a blue dish. I've got a whole closet full of them."

"*What?*" yells everybody. And then: "Will you sell 'em?"

"Sell 'em?" says Rogers, looking round surprised. "Why, I never see nothing I wouldn't sell if I got money enough for it."

Then for the next few minutes there was what old Parson Danvers used to call a study in human nature. All hands started for that poor, helpless plate owner as if they was going to swoop down on him like a passel of gulls on a dead horse-mack'rel. Then they come to themselves and stopped and looked at each other, kind of shame-faced but suspicious. The Duchess and her crowd glared at the Dowager tribe and got the glares back with compound interest. Everybody wanted to get Adoniram one side and talk with him, and everybody else was determined they shouldn't. Wherever he moved the "Antiquers" moved with him. Milo watched from the side lines. Rogers got scared.

"Look here," says he, staring sort of wild-like at the boarders. "What ails you folks? Are you crazy?"

Well, he might have made a good deal worse guess than that. I don't know how 'twould have ended if Peter T. Brown, cool and sassy as ever, hadn't come on deck just then and took command.

"See here, Rogers," he says, "let's understand this thing. Have you got a set of dishes like that?"

Adoniram looked at him. "Will I get jailed if I say yes ?" he answers.

"Maybe you will if you don't," says Peter. "Now, then, ladies and gentlemen, this is something we're all interested in, and I think everybody ought to have a fair show. I jedge from the defendant's testimony that he *has* got a set of the dishes, and I also jedge, from my experience and three years' dealings with him, that he's too public-spirited to keep 'em, provided he's paid four times what they're worth. Now my idea is this: Rogers will bring those dishes down here to-morrer and we'll put 'em on exhibition in the hotel parlor. Next day we'll have an auction and sell 'em to the highest cash bidder. And, provided there's no objection, I'll sacrifice my reputation and be auctioneer."

So 'twas agreed to have the auction.

Next day Adoniram heaves alongside with the dishes in a truck wagon, and they was strung out on the tables in the parlor. And such a pawing over and gabbling you never heard. I'd been supicious, myself, knowing Rogers, but there was the set from platters to sassers, and blue enough and ugly enough to be as antique as Mrs. Methusalem's jet earrings. The "Antiquers" handled 'em and admired 'em and p'inted to the three holes in the back of each dish—the same being proof of age—and got more covetous every minute. But the joy was limited. As one feller said, "I'd like 'em mighty well, but what chance'll we have bidding against green-back syndicates like that?" referring to the Dowager and the Duchess.

Milo and Eddie was the most worried of all, because each of 'em had been commissioned by their commanding officers not to let t'other family win.

That auction was the biggest thing that ever happened at the Old Home. We had it on the lawn out back of the billiard room and folks came from Harniss and Orham and the land knows where. The sheds and barn was filled with carriages and we served thirty-two extra dinners at a dollar a feed. The dishes was piled on a table and Peter T. done his auctioneer preaching from a kind of pulpit made out of two cracker boxes and a tea chest.

But there wa'n't any real bidding except from the Smalls and Thompsons. A few of the boarders and some of the out-of-towners took a shy long at first, but their bids was only ground bait. Milo and Eddie, backed by the Dowager and the Duchess, done the real fishing.

The price went up and up. Peter T. whooped and pounded and all but shed tears. If he'd been burying a competition hotel keeper he couldn't

have hove more soul into his work. 'Twas,
"Fifty! Do I hear sixty? Sixty do I hear? Fifty
dollars! *Think* of it? Why, friends, this ain't
a church pound party. Look at them dishes!
Look at 'em! Why, the pin feathers on those
blue dicky birds in the corners are worth more'n
that for mattress stuffing. Do I hear sixty?
Sixty I'm bid. Who says seventy?"

Milo said it, and Eddie was back at him afore
he could shake the reefs out of the last syllable.
She went up to a hundred, then to one hundred
and twenty-five, and with every raise Adoniram
Roger's smile lengthened out. After the one-
twenty-five mark the tide rose slower. Milo'd
raise it a dollar and Eddie'd jump him fifty
cents.

And just then two things happened. One
was that a servant girl come running from the
Old Home House to tell the Duchess and "Irene
dear" that some swell friends of theirs from the
hotel at Harniss had driven over to call and was
waiting for 'em in the parlor. The female Smalls
went in, though they wa'n't joyful over it. They
give Eddie his sailing orders afore they went, too.

The other thing that happened was Bill Saltmarsh's arriving in port. Bill is an "antiquer"
for revenue only. He runs an antique store
over at Ostable and the prices he charges are

enough to convict him without hearing the evidence. I knew he'd come.

Saltmarsh busts through the crowd and makes for the pulpit. He nods to Peter T. and picks up one of the plates. He looks at it first ruther casual; then more and more careful, turning it over and taking up another.

"Hold on a minute, Brown," says he. "Are *these* the dishes you're selling?"

"Sure thing," comes back Peter. "Think we're serving free lunch? No, sir! Those are the genuine articles, Mr. Saltmarsh, and you're cheating the widders and orphans if you don't put in a bid quick. One thirty-two fifty, I'm bid. Now, Saltmarsh!"

But Bill only laughed. Then he picks up another plate, looks at it, and laughs again.

"Good day, Brown," says he. "Sorry I can't stop." And off he puts towards his horse and buggy.

Eddie Small was watching him. Milo, being on the other side of the pulpit, hadn't noticed so partic'lar.

"Who's that?" asks Eddie, suspicious. "Does he know antiques?"

I remarked that if Bill didn't, then nobody did.

"Look here, Saltmarsh!" says Small, catching Bill by the arm as he shoved through the crowd.

"What's the matter with those dishes—anything?"

Bill turned and looked at him. "Why, no," he says, slow. "They're all right—of their kind." And off he put again.

But Eddie wa'n't satisfied. He turns to me. "By George!" he says. "What is it? Does he think they're fakes?"

I didn't know, so I shook my head. Small fidgetted, looked at Peter, and then run after Saltmarsh. Milo had just raised the bid.

"One hundred and thirty-three" hollers Peter, fetching the tea chest a belt. "One thirty-four do I hear? Make it one thirty-three fifty. Fifty cents do I hear? Come, come! this is highway robbery, gentlemen. Mr. Small—where are you?"

But Eddie was talking to Saltmarsh. In a minute back he comes, looking more worried than ever. Peter T. bawled and pounded and beckoned at him with the mallet, but he only fidgetted—didn't know what to do.

"One thirty-three!" bellers Peter. "One thirty-three! Oh, how can I look my grandmother's picture in the face after this? One thirty-three — once! One thirty-three — twice! Third and last call! One—thirty—"

Then Eddie begun to raise his hand, but 'twas too late.

"One thirty-three and SOLD! To Mr. Milo Thompson for one hundred and thirty-three dollars!"

And just then come a shriek from the piazza; the Duchess and "Irene dear" had come out of the parlor.

Well! Talk about crowing! The way that Thompson crowd rubbed it in on the Smalls was enough to make you leave the dinner table. They had the servants take in them dishes, piece by piece, and every single article, down to the last butter plate, was steered straight by the Small crowd.

As for poor Eddie, when he come up to explain why he hadn't kept on bidding, his wife put him out like he was a tin lamp.

"Don't *speak* to me!" says she. "Don't you *dare* speak to me."

He didn't dare. He just run up a storm sail and beat for harbor back of the barn. And from the piazza Milo cackled vainglorious.

Me and Cap'n Jonadab and Peter T. felt so sorry for Eddie, knowing what he had coming to him from the Duchess, that we went out to see him. He was setting on a wrecked hencoop, looking heart-broke but puzzled.

"'Twas that Saltmarsh made me lose my nerve," he says. "I thought when he wouldn't bid there was something wrong with the dishes. And there *was* something wrong, too. Now what was it?"

"Maybe the price was too high," says I.

"No, 'twa'n't that. I b'lieve yet he thought they were imitations. Oh, if they only were!"

And then, lo and behold you, around the corner comes Adoniram Rogers. I'd have bet large that whatever conscience Adoniram was born with had dried up and blown away years ago. But no; he'd resurrected a remnant.

"Mr. Small," stammered Mr. Rogers, "I'm sorry you feel bad about not buying them dishes. I—I thought I'd ought to tell you—that is to say, I— Well, if you want another set, I cal'late I can get it for you—that is, if you won't tell nobody."

"*Another* set?" hollers Eddie, wide-eyed. "Anoth— Do you mean to say you've got *more?*"

"Why, I ain't exactly got 'em now, but my nephew John keeps a furniture store in South Boston, and he has lots of sets like that. I bought that one off him."

Peter T. Brown jumps to his feet.

"Why, you outrageous robber!" he hollers. "Didn't you say those dishes were old?"

"I never said nothing, except that they were

like the plate that feller had on the piazza. And
they was, too. *You* folks said they was old, and
I thought you'd ought to know, so—"

Eddie Small threw up both hands. "Fakes!"
he hollers. "Fakes! *And Thompson paid one
hundred and thirty-three dollars for 'em!* Boys,
there's times when life's worth living. Have a
drink."

We went into the billard-room and took something; that is, Peter and Eddie took that kind
of something. Me and Jonadab took cigars.

"Fellers," said Eddie, "drink hearty. I'm
going in to tell my wife. Fake dishes! And I
beat Thompson on the davenport."

He went away bubbling like a biling spring.
After he was gone Rogers looked thoughtful.

"That's funny, too, ain't it ? " he says.

"What's funny ? " we asked.

"Why, about that sofy he calls a davenport.
You see, I bought that off John, too," says Adoniram.

HIS NATIVE HEATH

HIS NATIVE HEATH

I never could quite understand why the folks at Wellmouth made me selectman. I s'pose likely 'twas on account of Jonadab and me and Peter Brown making such a go of the Old Home House and turning Wellmouth Port from a sand fleas' paradise into a hospital where city folks could have their bank accounts amputated and not suffer more'n was necessary. Anyway, I was elected unanimous at town meeting, and Peter was mighty anxious for me to take the job.

"Barzilla," says Peter, "I jedge that a selectman is a sort of dwarf alderman. Now, I've had friends who've been aldermen, and they say it's a sure thing, like shaking with your own dice. If you're straight, there's the honor and the advertisement; if you're crooked, there's the graft. Either way the house wins. Go in, and glory be with you."

So I finally agreed to serve, and the very first meeting I went to, the question of Asaph Blueworthy and the poorhouse comes up. Zoeth Tiddit—he was town clerk—he puts it this way:

"Gentlemen," he says, "we have here the usual application from Asaph Blueworthy for aid from the town. I don't know's there's much use for me to read it—it's tolerable familiar. 'Suffering from lumbago and rheumatiz'—um, yes. 'Out of work'—um, just so. 'Respectfully begs that the board will'—etcetery and so forth. Well, gentlemen, what's your pleasure?"

Darius Gott, he speaks first, and dry and drawling as ever. "Out of work, hey?" says Darius. "Mr. Chairman, I should like to ask if anybody here remembers the time when Ase was *in* work?"

Nobody did, and Cap'n Benijah Poundberry —he was chairman at that time—he fetches the table a welt with his starboard fist and comes out emphatic.

"Feller members," says he, "I don't know how the rest of you feel, but it's my opinion that this board has done too much for that lazy loafer already. Long's his sister, Thankful, lived, we couldn't say nothing, of course. If she wanted to slave and work so's her brother could live in idleness and sloth, why, that was her business. There ain't any law against a body's making a fool of herself, more's the pity. But she's been dead a year, and he's done nothing since but live on those that'll trust him, and ask help from the town. He ain't sick—except sick of work. Now, it's my idea that, long's he's bound to be a pauper, he might's well be treated as a pauper. Let's send him to the poorhouse."

"But," says I, "he owns his place down there by the shore, don't he?"

All hands laughed—that is, all but Cap'n Benijah. "Own nothing," says the cap'n. "The whole rat trap, from the keel to maintruck, ain't worth more'n three hundred dollars, and I loaned Thankful four hundred on it years ago, and the mortgage fell due last September. Not a cent of principal, interest, nor rent have I got since, Whether he goes to the poorhouse or not, he goes out of that house of mine to-morrer. A man can smite me on one cheek and maybe I'll turn t'other, but when, after I *have* turned it, he finds fault 'cause my face hurts his hand, then I rise up and quit; you hear *me!*"

Nobody could help hearing him, unless they was deefer than the feller that fell out of the balloon and couldn't hear himself strike, so all hands agreed that sending Asaph Blueworthy to the poorhouse would be a good thing. 'Twould be a lesson to Ase, and would give the poorhouse one more excuse for being on earth. Wellmouth's a fairly prosperous town, and the paupers had died, one after the other, and no new ones had come, until all there was left in the poorhouse was old Betsy Mullen, who was down with creeping palsy, and Deborah Badger, who'd been keeper ever since her husband died.

The poorhouse property was valuable, too, 'specially for a summer cottage, being out on the end of Robbin's Point, away from the town, and having a fine view right across the bay. Zoeth Tiddit was a committee of one with power from the town to sell the place, but he hadn't found a customer yet. And if he did sell it, what to do with Debby was more or less of a question. She'd kept poorhouse for years, and had no other home nor no relations to go to. Everybody liked her, too—that is, everybody but Cap'n Benijah. He was down on her 'cause she was a Spiritualist and believed in fortune tellers and such. The cap'n, bein' a deacon of the Come-Outer persuasion, was naturally down on folks who wasn't broad-minded enough to see that his partic'lar crack in the roof was the only way to crawl through to glory.

Well, we voted to send Asaph to the poorhouse, and then I was appointed a delegate to see him and tell him he'd got to go. I wasn't enthusiastic over the job, but everybody said I was exactly the feller for the place.

"To tell you the truth," drawls Darius, "you, being a stranger, are the only one that Ase couldn't talk over. He's got a tongue that's buttered on both sides and runs on ball bearings. If I should see him he'd work on my sympathies till I'd lend him the last two-cent piece in my baby's bank."

So, as there wa'n't no way out of it, I drove down to Asaph's that afternoon. He lived off on a side road by the shore, in a little, run-down shanty that was as no account as he was. When I moored my horse to the "heavenly-wood" tree by what was left of the fence, I would have bet my sou'wester that I caught a glimpse of Brother Blueworthy, peeking round the corner of the house. But when I turned that corner there was nobody in sight, although the bu'sted wash-bench, with a cranberry crate propping up its lame end, was shaking a little, as if some one had set on it recent.

I knocked on the door, but nobody answered. After knocking three or four times, I tried kicking, and the second kick raised, from somewheres inside, a groan that was as lonesome a sound as ever I heard. No human noise in my experience come within a mile of it for dead, downright misery—unless, maybe, it's Cap'n Jonadab trying to sing in meeting Sundays.

"Who's that?" wails Ase from 'tother side of the door. "Did anybody knock?"

"Knock!" says I. "I all but kicked your everlasting derelict out of water. It's me, Wingate—one of the selectmen. Tumble up, there! I want to talk to you."

Blueworthy didn't exactly tumble, so's to speak, but the door opened, and he comes shuffling and groaning into sight. His face was twisted up and he had one hand spread-fingered on the small of his back.

"Dear, dear!" says he. "I'm dreadful sorry to have kept you waiting, Mr. Wingate. I've been wrastling with this turrible lumbago, and I'm 'fraid it's affecting my hearing. I'll tell you——"

"Yes—well, you needn't mind," I says; "'cordin' to common tell, you was born with that same kind of lumbago, and it's been getting no better fast ever since. Jest drag your sufferings out onto this bench and come to anchor. I've got considerable to say, and I'm in a hurry."

Well, he grunted, and groaned, and scuffled along. When he'd got planted on the bench he didn't let up any—kept on with the misery.

"Look here," says I, losing patience, "when you get through with the Job business I'll heave ahead and talk. Don't let me interrupt the lamentations on no account. Finished? All right. Now, you listen to me."

And then I told him just how matters stood. His house was to be seized on the mortgage, and he was to move to the poorhouse next day. You never see a man more surprised or worse cut up. Him to the poorhouse? *Him*—one of the oldest families on the Cape? You'd think he was the Grand Panjandrum. Well, the dignity didn't work, so he commenced on the lumbago; and that didn't work, neither. But do you think he give up the ship? Not much; he commenced to explain why he hadn't been able to earn a living and the reasons why he'd ought to have another chance. Talk! Well, if I hadn't been warned he'd have landed *me*, all right. I never heard a better sermon nor one with more long words in it.

I actually pitied him. It seemed a shame that a feller who could argue like that should have to go to the poorhouse; he'd ought to run a summer hotel—when the boarders kicked 'cause there was yeller-eyed beans in the coffee he would be the one to explain that they was lucky to get beans like that without paying extra for 'em. Thinks I, "I'm an idiot, but I'll make him one more offer."

So I says: "See here, Mr. Blueworthy, I could use another man in the stable at the Old Home House. If you want the job you can have it. *Only,* you'll have to work, and work hard."

Well, sir, would you believe it?—his face fell like a cook-book cake. That kind of chance wa'n't what he was looking for. He shuffled and hitched around, and finally he says: "I'll—I'll consider your offer," he says.

That was too many for me. "Well, I'll be yardarmed!" says I, and went off and left him "considering." I don't know what his considerations amounted to. All I know is that next day they took him to the poorhouse.

And from now on this yarn has got to be more or less hearsay. I'll have to put this and that together, like the woman that made the mince meat. Some of the facts I got from a cousin of Deborah Badger's, some of them I wormed out of Asaph himself one time when he'd had a jug come down from the city and was feeling toler'ble philanthropic and conversationy. But I guess they're straight enough.

Seems that, while I was down notifying Blue-worthy, Cap'n Poundberry had gone over to the poorhouse to tell the Widow Badger about her new boarder. The widow was glad to hear the news.

"He'll be somebody to talk to, at any rate," says she. "Poor old Betsy Mullen ain't exactly what you'd call company for a sociable body. But I'll mind what you say, Cap'n Benijah. It takes more than a slick tongue to come it over me. I'll make that lazy man work or know the reason why."

So when Asaph arrived—per truck wagon— at three o'clock the next afternoon, Mrs. Badger was ready for him. She didn't wait to shake hands or say: "Glad to see you." No, sir! The minute he landed she sent him out by the barn with orders to chop a couple of cords of oak slabs that was piled there. He groaned and commenced to develop lumbago symptoms, but she cured 'em in a hurry by remarking that her doctor's book said vig'rous exercise was the best physic for that kind of disease, and so he must chop hard. She waited till she heard the ax "chunk" once or twice, and then she went into the house, figgering that she'd gained the first lap, anyhow.

But in an hour or so it come over her all of a sudden that 'twas awful quiet out by the wood- pile. She hurried to the back door, and there was Ase, setting on the ground in the shade, his eyes shut and his back against the chopping block, and one poor lonesome slab in front of him with a couple of splinters knocked off it. That was his afternoon's work.

Maybe you think the widow wa'n't mad. She tip-toed out to the wood-pile, grabbed her new boarder by the coat collar and shook him till his head played "Johnny Comes Marching Home" against the chopping block.

"You lazy thing, you!" says she, with her eyes snapping. "Wake up and tell me what you mean by sleeping when I told you to work."

"Sleep?" stutters Asaph, kind of reaching out with his mind for a life-preserver. "I—I wa'n't asleep."

Well, I don't think he had really meant to sleep. I guess he just set down to think of a good brand new excuse for not working and kind of drowsed off.

"You wa'n't hey?" says Deborah. "Then 'twas the best imitation ever I see. What *was* you doing, if 'tain't too personal a question?"

"I—I guess I must have fainted. I'm subject to such spells. You see, ma'am, I ain't been well for——"

"Yes, I know. I understand all about that. Now, you march your boots into that house, where I can keep an eye on you, and help me get supper. To-morrer morning you'll get up at five o'clock and chop wood till breakfast time. If I think you've chopped enough, maybe you'll

THAT WAS HIS AFTERNOON'S WORK.

get the breakfast. If I don't think so you'll keep on chopping. Now, march!"

Blueworthy, he marched, but 'twa'n't as joyful a parade as an Odd Fellers' picnic. He could see he'd made a miscue—a clean miss, and the white ball in the pocket. He knew, too, that a lot depended on his making a good impression the first thing, and instead of that he'd gone and "foozled his approach," as that city feller said last summer when he ran the catboat plump into the end of the pier. Deborah, she went out into the kitchen, but she ordered Ase to stay in the dining room and set the table; told him to get the dishes out of the closet.

All the time he was doing it he kept thinking about the mistake he'd made, and wondering if there wa'n't some way to square up and get solid with the widow. Asaph was a good deal of a philosopher, and his motto was—so he told me afterward, that time I spoke of when he'd been investigating the jug—his motto was: "Every hard shell has a soft spot somewheres, and after you find it, it's easy." If he could only find out something that Deborah Badger was particular interested in, then he believed he could make a ten-strike. And, all at once, down in the corner of the closet, he see a big pile of papers and magazines. The one on top was the *Banner of Light*, and underneath that was the *Mysterious Magazine*.

Then he remembered, all of a sudden, the town talk about Debby's believing in mediums and spooks and fortune tellers and such. And he commenced to set up and take notice.

At the supper table he was as mum as a rundown clock; just set in his chair and looked at Mrs. Badger. She got nervous and fidgety after a spell, and fin'lly bu'sts out with: "What are you staring at me like that for?"

Ase kind of jumped and looked surprised. "Staring?" says he. "Was I staring?"

"I should think you was! Is my hair coming down, or what is it?"

He didn't answer for a minute, but he looked over her head and then away acrost the room, as if he was watching something that moved. "Your husband was a short, kind of fleshy man, as I remember, wa'n't he?" says he, absent-minded like.

"Course he was. But what in the world——"

"'Twa'n't him, then. I thought not."

"*Him?* My husband? What *do* you mean?"

And then Asaph begun to put on the fine touches. He leaned acrost the table and says he, in a sort of mysterious whisper: "Mrs. Badger," says he, "do you ever see things? Not common things, but strange—shadders like?"

"Mercy me!" says the widow. "No. Do *you?*"

"Sometimes seems's if I did. Jest now, as I set here looking at you, it seemed as if I saw a man come up and put his hand on your shoulder."

Well, you can imagine Debby. She jumped out of her chair and whirled around like a kitten in a fit. "Good land!" she hollers. "Where? What? Who was it?"

"I don't know who 'twas. His face was covered up; but it kind of come to me—a communication, as you might say—that some day that man was going to marry you."

"Land of love! Marry *me?* You're crazy! I'm scart to death."

Ase shook his head, more mysterious than ever. "I don't know," says he. "Maybe I am crazy. But I see that same man this afternoon, when I was in that trance, and——"

"Trance! Do you mean to tell me you was in a *trance* out there by the wood-pile? Are you a *medium?*"

Well, Ase, he wouldn't admit that he was a medium exactly, but he give her to understand that there wa'n't many mediums in this country that could do business 'longside of him when he was really working. 'Course he made believe he didn't want to talk about such things, and, likewise of course, that made Debby all the more anxious *to* talk about 'em. She found out that her new boarder was subject to trances and had second-sight and could draw horoscopes, and I don't know what all. Particular she wanted to

know more about that "man" that was going
to marry her, but Asaph wouldn't say much about
him.

"All I can say is," says Ase, "that he didn't
appear to me like a common man. He was sort
of familiar looking, and yet there was something
distinguished about him, something uncommon,
as you might say. But this much comes to me
strong: He's a man any woman would be proud
to get, and some time he's coming to offer you a
good home. You won't have to keep poorhouse
all your days."

So the widow went up to her room with what
you might call a case of delightful horrors. She
was too scart to sleep and frightened to stay awake.
She kept two lamps burning all night.

As for Asaph, he waited till 'twas still, and then
he crept downstairs to the closet, got an armful
of *Banners of Light* and *Mysterious Magazines*,
and went back to his room to study up. Next
morning there was nothing said about wood chopping—Ase was busy making preparations to draw
Debby's horoscope.

You can see how things went after that. Blueworthy was star boarder at that poorhouse. Mrs.
Badger was too much interested in spooks and
fortunes to think of asking him to work, and if
she did hint at such a thing, he'd have another

"trance" and see that "man," and 'twas all off. And we poor fools of selectmen was congratulating ourselves that Ase Blueworthy was doing something toward earning his keep at last. And then—'long in July 'twas—Betsy Mullen died.

One evening, just after the Fourth, Deborah and Asaph was in the dining room, figgering out fortunes with a pack of cards, when there comes a knock at the door. The widow answered it, and there was an old chap, dressed in a blue suit, and a stunning pretty girl in what these summer women make believe is a sea-going rig. And both of 'em was sopping wet through, and as miserable as two hens in a rain barrel.

It turned out that the man's name was Lamont, with a colonel's pennant and a million-dollar mark on the foretop of it, and the girl was his daughter Mabel. They'd been paying six dollars a day each for sea air and clam soup over to the Wattagonsett House, in Harniss, and either the soup or the air had affected the colonel's head till he imagined he could sail a boat all by his ownty-donty. Well, he'd sailed one acrost the bay and got becalmed, and then the tide took him in amongst the shoals at the mouth of Wellmouth Crick, and there, owing to a mix-up of tide, shoals, dark, and an overdose of foolishness, the boat had upset and foundered and the Lamonts had waded half a mile or so to shore. Once on dry land, they'd headed up the bluff for the only port in sight, which was the poorhouse—although they didn't know it.

The widow and Asaph made 'em as comfortable as they could; rigged 'em up in dry clothes which had belonged to departed paupers, and got 'em something to eat. The Lamonts was what they called "enchanted" with the whole establishment.

"This," says the colonel, with his mouth full of brown bread, "is delightful, really delightful. The New England hospitality that we read about. So free from ostentation and conventionality."

When you stop to think of it, you'd scurcely expect to run acrost much ostentation at the poorhouse, but, of course, the colonel didn't know, and he praised everything so like Sam Hill, that the widow was ashamed to break the news to him. And Ase kept quiet, too, you can be sure of that. As for Mabel, she was one of them gushy, goo-gooey kind of girls, and she was as struck with the shebang as her dad. She said the house itself was a "perfect dear."

And after supper they paired off and got to talking, the colonel with Mrs. Badger, and Asaph with Mabel. Now, I can just imagine how Ase talked to that poor, unsuspecting young female. He sartin did love an audience, and here was one that didn't know him nor his history, nor nothing. He played the sad and mysterious. You could see that he was a blighted bud, all right. He was a man with a hidden sorrer, and the way he'd sigh and change the subject when it come to embarrassing questions was enough to bring tears to a graven image, let alone a romantic girl just out of boarding school.

Then, after a spell of this, Mabel wanted to be shown the house, so as to see the "sweet, old-fashioned rooms." And she wanted papa to see 'em, too, so Ase led the way, like the talking man in the dime museum. And the way them Lamonts agonized over every rag mat, and corded bedstead was something past belief. When they was saying good-night—they *had* to stay all night because their own clothes wa'n't dry and those they had on were more picturesque than stylish—Mabel turns to her father and says she:

"Papa, dear," she says, "I believe that at last we've found the very thing we've been looking for."

And the colonel said yes, he guessed they had.

Next morning they was up early and out enjoying the view; it *is* about the best view alongshore, and they had a fit over it. When breakfast was done the Lamonts takes Asaph one side and the colonel says:

"Mr. Blueworthy," he says, "my daughter and I am very much pleased with the Cape and the Cape people. Some time ago we made up our minds that if we could find the right spot we would build a summer home here. Preferably we wish to purchase a typical, old-time, Colonial homestead and remodel it, retaining, of course, all the original old-fashioned flavor. Cost is not so much the consideration as location and the house itself. We are—ahem!—well, frankly, your place here suits us exactly."

"We adore it," says Mabel, emphatic.

"Mr. Blueworthy," goes on the colonel, "will you sell us your home? I am prepared to pay a liberal price."

Poor Asaph was kind of throwed on his beam ends, so's to speak. He hemmed and hawed, and finally had to blurt out that he didn't own the place. The Lamonts was astonished. The colonel wanted to know if it belonged to Mrs. Badger.

"Why, no," says Ase. "The fact is—that is to say—you see——"

And just then the widow opened the kitchen window and called to 'em.

"Colonel Lamont," says she, "there's a sailboat beating up the harbor, and I think the folks on it are looking for you."

The colonel excused himself, and run off down the hill toward the back side of the point, and Asaph was left alone with the girl. He see, I s'pose, that here was his chance to make the best yarn out of what was bound to come out anyhow in a few minutes. So he fetched a sigh that sounded as if 'twas racking loose the foundations and commenced.

He asked Mabel if she was prepared to hear something that would shock her turrible, something that would undermine her confidence in human natur'. She was a good deal upset, and no wonder, but she braced up and let on that she guessed she could stand it. So then he told her that her dad and her had been deceived, that that house wa'n't his nor Mrs. Badger's; 'twas the Wellmouth poor farm, and he was a pauper.

She was shocked, all right enough, but afore she had a chance to ask a question, he begun to tell her the story of his life. 'Twas a fine chance for him to spread himself, and I cal'late he done it to the skipper's taste. He told her how him and his sister had lived in their little home, their own little nest, over there by the shore, for years and years. He led her out to where she could see the roof of his old shanty over the sand hills, and he wiped his eyes and raved over it. You'd think that tumble-down shack was a hunk out of paradise; Adam and Eve's place in the Garden was a short lobster 'longside of it. Then, he said, he was took down with an incurable disease. He tried and tried to get along, but 'twas no go. He mortgaged the shanty to a grasping money lender—meanin' Poundberry— and that money was spent. Then his sister passed away and his heart broke; so they took him to the poorhouse.

"Miss Lamont," says he, "good-by. Sometimes in the midst of your fashionable career, in your gayety and so forth, pause," he says, "and give a thought to the broken-hearted pauper who has told you his life tragedy."

Well, now, you take a green girl, right fresh from novels and music lessons, and spring that on her—what can you expect? Mabel, she cried and took on dreadful.

"Oh, Mr. Blueworthy!" says she, grabbing his hand. "I'm *so* glad you told me. I'm *so* glad! Cheer up," she says. "I respect you more than ever, and my father and I will——"

Just then the colonel comes puffing up the hill. He looked as if he'd heard news.

"My child," he says in a kind of horrified whisper, "can you realize that we have actually passed the night in the—in the *almshouse?*"

Mabel held up her hand. "Hush, papa,"

she says. "Hush. I know all about it. Come
away, quick; I've got something very important to say to you."

And she took her dad's arm and went off down
the hill, mopping her pretty eyes with her hand-
kerchief and smiling back, every once in a while,
through her tears, at Asaph.

Now, it happened that there was a selectmen's
meeting that afternoon at four o'clock. I was
on hand, and so was Zoeth Tiddit and most of
the others. Cap'n Poundberry and Darius Gott
were late. Zoeth was as happy as a clam at high
water; he'd sold the poorhouse property that
very day to a Colonel Lamont, from Harniss,
who wanted it for a summer place.

"And I got the price we set on it, too," says
Zoeth. "But that wa'n't the funniest part of it.
Seems's old man Lamont and his daughter was
very much upset because Debby Badger and Ase
Blueworthy would be turned out of house and
home 'count of the place being sold. The colonel was hot foot for giving 'em a check for five
hundred dollars to square things; said his daughter'd made him promise he would. Says I:
'You can give it to Debby, if you want to, but
don't lay a copper on that Blueworthy fraud.'
Then I told him the truth about Ase. He couldn't
hardly believe it, but I finally convinced him,

and he made out the check to Debby. I took it down to her myself just after dinner. Ase was there, and his eyes pretty nigh popped out of his head.

"'Look here,' I says to him; 'if you'd been worth a continental you might have had some of this. As it is, you'll be farmed out somewheres —that's what'll happen to *you*.'"

And as Zoeth was telling this, in comes Cap'n Benijah. He was happy, too.

"I cal'late the Lamonts must be buying all the property alongshore," he says when he heard the news. "I sold that old shack that I took from Blueworthy to that Lamont girl to-day for three hundred and fifty dollars. She wouldn't say what she wanted of it, neither, and I didn't care much; *I* was glad to get rid of it."

"*I* can tell you what she wanted of it," says somebody behind us. We turned round and 'twas Gott; he'd come in. "I just met Squire Foster," he says, "and the squire tells me that that Lamont girl come into his office with the bill of sale for the property you sold her and made him deed it right over to Ase Blueworthy, as a present from her."

"*What?*" says all hands, Poundberry loudest of all.

"That's right," said Darius. "She told the

squire a long rigamarole about what a martyr Ase was, and how her dad was going to do something for him, but that she was going to give him his home back again with her own money, money her father had given her to buy a ring with, she said, though that ain't reasonable, of course—nobody'd pay that much for a ring. The squire tried to tell her what a no-good Ase was, but she froze him quicker'n— Where you going, Cap'n Benije ?"

"I'm going down to that poorhouse," hollers Poundberry. "I'll find out the rights and wrongs of this thing mighty quick."

We all said we'd go with him, and we went, six in one carryall. As we hove in sight of the poorhouse a buggy drove away from it, going in t'other direction.

"That looks like the Baptist minister's buggy," says Darius. "What on earth's he been down here for ? "

Nobody could guess. As we run alongside the poorhouse door, Ase Blueworthy stepped out, leading Debby Badger. She was as red as an auction flag.

"By time, Ase Blueworthy!" hollers Cap'n Benijah, starting to get out of the carryall, "what do you mean by—— Debby, what are you holding that rascal's hand for ? "

But Ase cut him short. "Cap'n Poundberry," says he, dignified as a boy with a stiff neck, "I might pass over your remarks to me, but when you address my wife——"

"Your *wife?*" hollers everybody—everybody but the cap'n; he only sort of gurgled.

"My wife," says Asaph. "When you men—church members, too, some of you—sold the house over her head, I'm proud to say that I, having a home once more, was able to step for'ard and ask her to share it with me. We was married a few minutes ago," he says.

"And, oh, Cap'n Poundberry!" cried Debby, looking as if this was the most wonderful part of it—"oh, Cap'n Poundberry!" she says, "we've known for a long time that some man—an uncommon kind of man—was coming to offer me a home some day, but even Asaph didn't know 'twas himself; did you, Asaph?"

We selectmen talked the thing over going home, but Cap'n Benijah didn't speak till we was turning in at his gate. Then he fetched his knee a thump with his fist, and says he, in the most disgusted tone ever I heard:

"A house and lot for nothing," he says, "a wife to do the work for him, and five hundred dollars to spend! Sometimes the way this world's run gives me moral indigestion."

Which was tolerable radical for a Come-Outer to say, seems to me.

JONESY

JONESY

'Twas Peter T. Brown that suggested it, you might know. And, as likewise you might know, 'twas Cap'n Jonadab that done the most of the growling.

"They ain't no sense in it, Peter," says he. "Education's all right in its place, but 'tain't no good out of it. Why, one of my last voyages in the schooner *Samuel Emory*, I had a educated cook, feller that had graduated from one of them correspondence schools. He had his diploma framed and hung up on the wall of the galley along with tintypes of two or three of his wives, and pictures cut out of the *Police News*, and the like of that. And cook! Why, say! one of the fo'mast hands ate half a dozen of that cook's saleratus biscuit and fell overboard. If he hadn't been tangled up in his cod line, so we could haul him up by that, he'd have been down yet. He'd never have riz of his own accord, not with them biscuits in him. And as for his pie! the mate ate one of them bakeshop paper plates one time, thinking 'twas under crust; and he kept sayin' how unusual tender 'twas, at that. Now, what good was education to that cook? Why——"

"Cut it out!" says Peter T., disgusted. "Who's talking about cooks? These fellers ain't cooks— they're——"

"I know. They're waiters. Now, there 'tis again. When I give an order and there's any back talk, I want to understand it. You take a passel of college fellers, like you want to hire for waiters. S'pose I tell one of 'em to do something, and he answers back in Greek or Hindoo, or such. *I* can't tell what he says. I sha'n't know whether to bang him over the head or give him a cigar. What's the matter with the waiters we had last year? They talked Irish, of course, but I understood the most of that, and when I didn't 'twas safe to roll up my sleeves and begin arguing. But——"

"Oh, ring off!" says Peter. "Twenty-three!"

And so they had it, back and forth. I didn't say nothing. I knew how 'twould end. If Peter T. Brown thought 'twas good judgment to hire a mess of college boys for waiters, fellers who could order up the squab in pigeon-English and the ham in hog-Latin, I didn't care, so long as the orders and boarders got filled and the payroll didn't have growing pains. I had considerable faith in Brown's ideas, and he was as set on this one as a Brahma hen on a plaster nest-egg.

"It'll give tone to the shebang," says he, referring to the hotel; "and we want to keep the Old Home House as high-toned as a ten-story organ factory. And as for education, that's a matter of taste. Me, I'd just as soon have a waiter that bashfully admitted 'Wee, my dam,' as I would one that pushed 'Shur-r-e, Moike!' edgeways out of one corner of his mouth and served the lettuce on top of the lobster, from principle, to keep the green above the red. When it comes to tone and tin, Cap'n, you trust your Uncle Pete; he hasn't been sniffling around the tainted-money bunch all these days with a cold in his head."

So it went his way finally, as I knew it would, and when the Old Home opened up on June first, the college waiters was on hand. And they was as nice a lot of boys as ever handled plates and wiped dishes for their board and four dollars a week. They was poor, of course, and working their passage through what they called the "varsity," but they attended to business and wa'n't a mite set up by their learning.

And they made a hit with the boarders, espe-

cially the women folks. Take the crankiest
old battle ship that ever cruised into breakfast
with diamond headlights showing and a pretty
daughter in tow, and she would eat lumpy oat-
meal and scorched eggs and never sound a distress
signal. How could she, with one of them nice-
looking gentlemanly waiters hanging over her
starboard beam and purring, "Certainly, madam,"
and "Two lumps or one, madam?" into her
ear? Then, too, she hadn't much time to find
fault with the grub, having to keep one eye on
the daughter. The amount of complaints that
them college boys saved in the first fortnight
was worth their season's wages, pretty nigh.
Before June was over the Old Home was full
up and we had to annex a couple of next-door
houses for the left-overs.

I was skipper for one of them houses, and Jonadab
run the other. Each of us had a cook and a
waiter, a housekeeper and an up-stairs girl. My
housekeeper was the boss prize in the package.
Her name was Mabel Seabury, and she was
young and quiet and as pretty as the first bunch
of Mayflowers in the spring. And a lady—
whew! The first time I set opposite to her at
table I made up my mind I wouldn't drink out
of my sasser if I scalded the lining off my throat.
She was city born and brought up, but she

wa'n't one of your common "He! he! ain't you turrible!" lunch-counter princesses, with a head like a dandelion gone to seed and a fish-net waist. You bet she wa'n't! Her dad had had money once, afore he tried to beat out Jonah and swallow the stock exchange whale. After that he was skipper of a little society library up to Cambridge, and she kept house for him. Then he died and left her his blessing, and some of Peter Brown's wife's folks, that knew her when she was well off, got her the job of housekeeper here with us.

The only trouble she made was first along, and that wa'n't her fault. I thought at one time we'd have to put up a wire fence to keep them college waiters away from her. They hung around her like a passel of gulls around a herring boat. She was nice to 'em, too, but when you're just so nice to everybody and not nice enough to any special one, the prospect ain't encouraging. So they give it up, but there wa'n't a male on the place, from old Dr. Blatt, mixer of Blatt's Burdock Bitters and Blatt's Balm for Beauty, down to the boy that emptied the ashes, who wouldn't have humped himself on all fours and crawled eight miles if she'd asked him to. And that includes me and Cap'n Jonadab, and we're about as tough a couple of women-proof old hulks as you'll find afloat.

Jonadab took a special interest in her. It pretty nigh broke his heart to think she was running my house instead of his. He thought she'd ought to be married and have a home of her own.

"Well," says I, "why don't she get married then? She could drag out and tie up any single critter of the right sex in this neighborhood with both hands behind her back."

"Humph!" says he. "I s'pose you'd have her marry one of these soup-toting college chaps, wouldn't you? Then they could live on Greek for breakfast and Latin for dinner and warm over the leavings for supper. No, sir! a girl hasn't no right to get married unless she gets a man with money. There's a deck-load of millionaires comes here every summer, and I'm goin' to help her land one of 'em. It's my duty as a Christian," says he.

One evening, along the second week in July 'twas, I got up from the supper-table and walked over toward the hotel, smoking, and thinking what I'd missed in not having a girl like that set opposite me all these years. And, in the shadder of the big bunch of lilacs by the gate, I see a feller standing, a feller with a leather bag in his hand, a stranger

"Good evening," says I. "Looking for the hotel, was you?"

He swung round, kind of lazy-like, and looked at me. Then I noticed how big he was. Seemed to me he was all of seven foot high and broad according. And rigged up—my soul! He had on a wide, felt hat, with a whirligig top onto it, and a light checked suit, and gloves, and slung more style than a barber on Sunday. If *I'd* wore them kind of duds they'd have had me down to Danvers, clanking chains and picking straws, but on this young chap they looked fine.

"Good evening," says the seven-footer, looking down and speaking to me cheerful. "Is this the Old Ladies' Home—the Old Home House, I should say?"

"Yes, sir," says I, looking up reverent at that hat.

"Right," he says. "Will you be good enough to tell me where I can find the proprietor?"

"Well," says I, "I'm him; that is, I'm one of him. But I'm afraid we can't accommodate you, mister, not now. We ain't got a room nowheres that ain't full."

He knocked the ashes off his cigarette. "I'm not looking for a room," says he, "except as a side issue. I'm looking for a job."

"A job!" I sings out. "A *job?*"

"Yes. I understand you employ college men as waiters. I'm from Harvard, and ——"

"A waiter?" I says, so astonished that I could hardly swaller. "Be you a waiter?"

"*I* don't know. I've been told so. Our coach used to say I was the best waiter on the team. At any rate I'll try the experiment."

Soon's ever I could gather myself together I reached across and took hold of his arm.

"Son," says I, ":you come with me and turn in. You'll feel better in the morning. I don't know where I'll put you, unless it's the bowling alley, but I guess that's your size. You oughtn't to get this way at your age."

He laughed a big, hearty laugh, same as I like to hear. "It's straight," he says. "I mean it. I want a job."

"But what for? You ain't short of cash?"

"You bet!" he says. "Strapped."

"Then," says I, "you come with me to-night and to-morrer morning you go somewheres and sell them clothes you've got on. You'll make more out of that than you will passing pie, if you passed it for a year."

He laughed again, but he said he was bound to be a waiter and if I couldn't help him he'd have to hunt up the other portion of the proprietor. So I told him to stay where he was, and I went off and found Peter T. You'd ought to seen Peter stare when we hove in sight of the candidate.

"Thunder!" says he. "Is this Exhibit One, Barzilla? Where'd you pick up the Chinese giant?"

I done the polite, mentioning Brown's name hesitating on t'other chap's.

"Er-Jones," says the human lighthouse. "Er-yes; Jones."

"Glad to meet you, Mr. Jones," says Peter. "So you want to be a waiter, do you? For how much per?"

"Oh, I don't know. I'll begin at the bottom, being a green hand. Twenty a week or so; whatever you're accustomed to paying."

Brown choked. "The figure's all right," he says, "only it covers a month down here."

"Right!" says Jones, not a bit shook up. "A month goes."

Peter stepped back and looked him over, beginning with the tan shoes and ending with the whirligig hat.

"Jonesy," says he, finally, "you're on. Take him to the servants' quarters, Wingate."

A little later, when I had the chance and had Brown alone, I says to him:

"Peter," says I, "for the land sakes what did you hire the emperor for? A blind man could see *he* wa'n't no waiter. And we don't need him anyhow; no more'n a cat needs three tails. Why——"

But he was back at me before I could wink. "Need him?" he says. "Why, Barzilla, we need him more than the old Harry needs a conscience. Take a bird's-eye view of him! Size him up! He puts all the rest of the Greek statues ten miles in the shade. If I could only manage to get his picture in the papers we'd have all the romantic old maids in Boston down here inside of a week; and there's enough of *them* to keep one hotel going till judgment. Need him? Whew!"

Next morning we was at the breakfast-table in my branch establishment, me and Mabel and the five boarders. All hands was doing their best to start a famine in the fruit market, and Dr. Blatt was waving a banana and cheering us with a yarn about an old lady that his Burdock Bitters had h'isted bodily out of the tomb. He was at the most exciting part, the bitters and the undertaker coming down the last lap neck and neck, and an even bet who'd win the patient, when the kitchen door opens and in marches the waiter with the tray full of dishes of "cereal." Seems to me 'twas chopped hay we had that morning—either that or shavings; I always get them breakfast foods mixed up.

But 'twa'n't the hay that made everybody set up and take notice. 'Twas the waiter himself.

Our regular steward was a spindling little critter with curls and eye-glasses who answered to the hail of "Percy." This fellow clogged up the scenery like a pet elephant, and was down in the shipping list as "Jones."

The doc left his invalid hanging on the edge of the grave, and stopped and stared. Old Mrs. Bounderby h'isted the gold-mounted double spy-glass she had slung round her neck and took an observation. Her daughter "Maizie" fetched a long breath and shut her eyes, like she'd seen her finish and was resigned to it.

"Well, Mr. Jones," says I, soon's I could get my breath, "this is kind of unexpected, ain't it? Thought you was booked for the main deck."

"Yes, sir," he says, polite as a sewing-machine agent, "I was, but Percy and I have exchanged. Cereal this morning, madam?"

Mrs. Bounderby took her measure of shavings and Jones's measure at the same time. She had him labeled "Danger" right off; you could tell that by the way she spread her wings over "Maizie." But I wa'n't watching her just then. I was looking at Mabel Seabury—looking and wondering.

The housekeeper was white as the tablecloth. She stared at the Jones man as if she couldn't believe her eyes, and her breath come short and quick. I thought sure she was going to cry. And what she ate of that meal wouldn't have made a lunch for a hearty humming-bird.

When 'twas finished I went out on the porch to think things over. The dining room winder was open and Jonesy was clearing the table. All of a sudden I heard him say, low and earnest:

"Well, aren't you going to speak to me?"

The answer was in a girl's voice, and I knew the voice. It said:

"You! *you!* How *could* you? Why did you come?"

"You didn't think I could stay away, did you?"

"But how did you know I was here? I tried *so* hard to keep it a secret."

"It took me a month, but I worked it out finally. Aren't you glad to see me?"

She burst out crying then, quiet, but as if her heart was hroke.

"Oh!" she sobs. "How could you be so cruel! And they've been so kind to me here."

I went away then, thinking harder than ever. At dinner Jonesy done the waiting, but Mabel wa'n't on deck. She had a headache, the cook said, and was lying down. 'Twas the same way at supper, and after supper Peter Brown comes to me, all broke up, and says he:

"There's merry clink to pay," he says. "Mabel's going to leave."

"No?" says I. "She ain't neither!"

"Yes, she is. She says she's going to-morrer. She won't tell me why, and I've argued with her for two hours. She's going to quit, and I'd rather enough sight quit myself. What'll we do?" says he.

I couldn't help him none, and he went away, moping and miserable. All round the place everybody was talking about the "lovely" new waiter, and to hear the girls go on you'd think the Prince of Wales had landed. Jonadab was the only kicker, and he said 'twas bad enough afore, but now that new dude had shipped, 'twa'n't the place for a decent, self-respecting man.

"How you goin' to order that Grand Panjandrum around?" he says. "Great land of Goshen! I'd as soon think of telling the Pope of Rome to empty a pail of swill as I would him. Why don't he stay to home and be a tailor's sign or something? Not prance around here with his high-toned airs. I'm glad you've got him, Barzilla, and not me."

Well, most of that was plain jealousy, so I didn't contradict. Besides I was too busy thinking. By eight o'clock I'd made up my mind and I went hunting for Jones.

I found him, after a while, standing by the back door and staring up at the chamber winders as if he missed something. I asked him to come along with me. Told him I had a big cargo of talk aboard, and wouldn't be able to cruise on an even keel till I'd unloaded some of it. So he fell into my wake, looking puzzled, and in a jiffy we was planted in the rocking chairs up in my bedroom.

"Look here," says I, "Mr.—Mr.——"

"Jones," says he.

"Oh, yes—Jones. It's a nice name."

"I remember it beautifully," says he, smiling.

"All right, Mr. Jones. Now, to begin with, we'll agree that it ain't none of my darn business, and I'm an old gray-headed nosey, and the like of that. But, being that I *am* old—old enough to be your dad, though that's my only recommend for the job—I'm going to preach a little sermon. My text is found in the Old Home Hotel, Wellmouth, first house on the left. It's Miss Seabury," says I.

He was surprised, I guess, but he never turned a hair. "Indeed?" he says. "She is the—the housekeeper, isn't she?"

"She was," says I, "but she leaves to-morrer morning."

That hit him between wind and water.

"No?" he sings out, setting up straight and staring at me. "Not really?"

"You bet," I says. "Now down in this part of the chart we've come to think more of that young lady than a cat does of the only kitten left out of the bag in the water bucket. Let me tell you about her."

So I went ahead, telling him how Mabel had come to us, why she come, how well she was liked, how much she liked us, and a whole lot more. I guess he knew the most of it, but he was too polite not to act interested.

"And now, all at once," says I, "she gives up being happy and well and contented, and won't eat, and cries, and says she's going to leave. There's a reason, as the advertisement folks say, and I'm going to make a guess at it. I believe it calls itself Jones."

His under jaw pushed out a little and his eyebrows drew together. But all he said was, "Well?"

"Yes," I says. "And now, Mr. Jones, I'm old, as I said afore, and nosey maybe, but I like that girl. Perhaps I might come to like you, too; you can't tell. Under them circumstances, and with the understanding that it didn't go no farther, maybe you might give me a glimpse of the lay of the land. Possibly I might have something to say that would help. I'm fairly white underneath, if I be sunburned. What do you think about it?"

He didn't answer right off; seemed to be chewing it over. After a spell he spoke.

"Mr. Wingate," says he, "with the understanding that you mentioned, I don't mind supposing a case. Suppose you was a chap in college. Suppose you met a girl in the vicinity that was—well, was about the best ever. Suppose you came to find that life wasn't worth a continental without that girl. Then suppose you had a dad with money, lots of money. Suppose the old fo—the gov'nor, I mean—without even seeing her or even knowing her name or a thing about her, said no. Suppose you and the old gentleman had a devil of a row, and broke off for keeps. Then suppose the girl wouldn't listen to you under the circumstances. Talked rot about 'wasted future' and 'throwing your life away' and so on. Suppose, when you showed her that you didn't care a red for futures, she ran away from you and wouldn't tell where she'd gone. Suppose—well, I guess that's enough supposing. I don't know why I'm telling you these things, anyway."

He stopped and scowled at the floor, acting like he was sorry he spoke. I pulled at my pipe a minute or so and then says I:

"Hum!" I says, "I presume likely it's fair to suppose that this break with the old gent is for good ?''

He didn't answer, but he didn't need to; the look on his face was enough.

"Yes," says I. "Well, it's likewise to be supposed that the idea—the eventual idea—is marriage, straight marriage, hey?"

He jumped out of his chair. "Why, damn you!" he says. "I'll——"

"All right. Set down and be nice. I was fairly sure of my soundings, but it don't do no harm to heave the lead. I ask your pardon. Well, what you going to support a wife on—her kind of a wife? A summer waiter's job at twenty a month?"

He set down, but he looked more troubled than ever. I was sorry for him; I couldn't help liking the boy.

"Suppose she keeps her word and goes away," says I. "What then?"

"I'll go after her."

"Suppose she still sticks to her principles and won't have you? Where'll you go, then?"

"To the hereafter," says he, naming the station at the end of the route.

"Oh, well, there's no hurry about that. Most of us are sure of a free one-way pass to that port some time or other, 'cording to the parson's tell. See here, Jones; let's look at this thing like a couple of men, not children. You don't want to keep chasing that girl from pillar to post, making her more miserable than she is now. And you ain't in no position to marry her. The way to show a young woman like her that you mean business and are going to be wuth cooking meals for is to get the best place you can and start in to earn a living and save money. Now, Mr. Brown's father-in-law is a man by the name of Dillaway, Dillaway of the Consolidated Cash Stores. He'll do things for me if I ask him to, and I happen to know that he's just started a branch up to Providence and is there now. Suppose I give you a note to him, asking him, as a favor to me, to give you the best job he can. He'll do it, I know. After that it's up to you. This is, of course, providing that you start for Providence to-morrer morning. What d'you say ? "

He was thinking hard. "Suppose I don't make good ? " he says. "I never worked in my life. And suppose she——"

"Oh, suppose your granny's pet hen hatched turkeys," I says, getting impatient, "I'll risk your making good. I wa'n't a first mate, shipping fo'mast hands ten years, for nothing. I can generally tell beet greens from cabbage without waiting to smell 'em cooking. And as for her, it seems to me that a girl who thinks enough of a feller to run away from him so's he won't spile his future, won't like him no less for being willing to work and wait for her. You stay here and think it over. I'm going out for a spell."

When I come back Jonesy was ready for me.

"Mr. Wingate," says he, "it's a deal. I'm going to go you, though I think you're plunging on a hundred-to-one shot. Some day I'll tell you more about myself, maybe. But now I'm going to take your advice and the position. I'll do my best, and I must say you're a brick. Thanks awfully."

"Good enough!" I says. "Now you go and tell her, and I'll write the letter to Dillaway."

So the next forenoon Peter T. Brown was joyful all up one side because Mabel had said she'd stay, and mournful all down the other because his pet college giant had quit almost afore he started. I kept my mouth shut, that being the best play I know of, nine cases out of ten.

I went up to the depot with Jonesy to see him off.

"Good-by, old man," he says, shaking hands. "You'll write me once in a while, telling me how she is, and—and so on?"

"Bet you!" says I. "I'll keep you posted up. And let's hear how you tackle the Consolidated Cash business."

July and the first two weeks in August moped along and everything at the Old Home House kept about the same. Mabel was in mighty good spirits, for her, and she got prettier every day. I had a couple of letters from Jones, saying that he guessed he could get bookkeeping through his skull in time without a surgical operation, and old Dillaway was down over one Sunday and was preaching large concerning the "find" my candidate was for the Providence branch. So I guessed I hadn't made no mistake.

I had considerable fun with Cap'n Jonadab over his not landing a rich husband for the Seabury girl. Looked like the millionaire crop was going to be a failure that summer.

"Aw, belay!" says he, short as baker's pie crust. "The season ain't over yet. You better take a bath in the salt mack'rel kag; you're too fresh to keep this hot weather."

Talking "husband" to him was like rubbing pain-killer on a scalded pup, so I had something to keep me interested dull days. But one morning he comes to me, excited as a mouse at a cat show, and says he:

"Ah, ha! what did I tell you? I've got one!"

"I see you have," says I. "Want me to send for the doctor?"

"Stop your foolishing," he says. "I mean

I've got a millionaire. He's coming to-night, too. One of the biggest big-bugs there is in New York. Ah, ha! what did I tell you?"

He was fairly boiling over with gloat, but from between the bubbles I managed to find out that the new boarder was a big banker from New York, name of Van Wedderburn, with a barrel of cash and a hogshead of dyspepsy. He was a Wall Street "bear," and a steady diet of lamb with mint sass had fetched him to where the doctors said 'twas lay off for two months or be laid out for keeps.

"And I've fixed it that he's to stop at your house, Barzilla," crows Jonadab. "And when he sees Mabel—well, you know what she's done to the other men folks," he says.

"Humph!" says I, "maybe he's got dyspepsy of the heart along with the other kind. She might disagree with him. What makes you so cock sartin?"

"'Cause he's a widower," he says. "Them's the softest kind."

"Well, you ought to know," I told him. "You're one yourself. But, from what I've heard, soft things are scarce in Wall Street. Bet you seventy-five cents to a quarter it don't work."

He wouldn't take me, having scruples against

betting—except when he had the answer in his pocket. But he went away cackling joyful, and that night Van Wedderburn arrived.

Van was a substantial-looking old relic, built on the lines of the Boston State House, broad in the beam and with a shiny dome on top. But he could qualify for the nervous dyspepsy class all right, judging by his langunge to the depot-wagon driver. When he got through making remarks because one of his trunks had been forgot, that driver's quotation, according to Peter T., had "dropped to thirty cents, with a second assessment called." I jedged the meals at our table would be as agreeable as a dog-fight.

However, 'twas up to me, and I towed him in and made him acquainted with Mabel. She wa'n't enthusiastic—having heard some of the driver sermon, I cal'late—until I mentioned his name. Then she gave a little gasp like. When Van had gone up to his rooms, puffing like a donkey-engyne and growling 'cause there wa'n't no elevators, she took me by the arm and says she:

"*What* did you say his name was, Mr. Wingate?"

"Van Wedderburn," says I. "The New York millionaire one."

"Not of Van Wedderburn & Hamilton, the bankers?" she asks, eager.

"That's him," says I. "Why? Do you know him? Did his ma used to do washing at your house?"

She laughed, but her face was all lit up and her eyes fairly shone. I could have—but there! never mind.

"Oh, no," she says, "I don't know him, but I know *of* him—everybody does."

Well, everybody did, that's a fact, and the way Marm Bounderby and Maizie was togged out at the supper-table was a sin and a shame. And the way they poured gush over that bald-headed broker was enough to make him slip out of his chair. Talk about "fishers of men"! them Bounderbys was a whole seiner's crew in themselves.

But what surprised me was Mabel Seabury. She was dressed up, too; not in the Bounderbys' style—collar-bones and diamonds—but in plain white with lace fuzz. If she wa'n't peaches and cream, then all you need is lettuce to make me a lobster salad.

And she was as nice to Van as if he was old Deuteronomy out of the Bible. He set down to that meal with a face on him like a pair of nutcrackers, and afore 'twas over he was laughing and eating apple pie and telling funny yarns about robbing his "friends" in the Street. I

judged he'd be sorry for it afore morning, but I
didn't care for that. I was kind of worried myself; didn't understand it.

And I understood it less and less as the days
went by. If she'd been Maizie Bounderby, with
two lines in each hand and one in her teeth,
she couldn't have done more to hook that old
stock-broker. She cooked little special dishes
for his dyspepsy to play with, and set with him
on the piazza evenings, and laughed at his jokes,
and the land knows what. Inside of a fortni't
he was a gone goose, which wa'n't surprising—
every other man being in the same fix—but 'twas
surprising to see her helping the goneness along.
All hands was watching the game, of course, and
it pretty nigh started a mutiny at the Old Home.
The Bounderbys packed up and lit out in ten
days, and none of the other women would speak
to Mabel. They didn't blame poor Mr. Van,
you understand. 'Twas all her—"low, design-
ing thing!"

And Jonadab! he wa'n't fit to live with. The
third forenoon after Van Wedderburn got there
he come around and took the quarter bet. And
the way he crowed over me made my hands
itch for a rope's end. Finally I owned up to
myself that I'd made a mistake; the girl was
a whitewashed tombstone and the whitewash

was rubbing thin. That night I dropped a line to poor Jonesy at Providence, telling him that, if he could get a day off, maybe he'd better come down to Wellmouth, and see to his fences; somebody was feeding cows in his pasture.

INSIDE OF A FORTNIGHT HE WAS A GONE GOOSE.

The next day was Labor Day, and what was left of the boarders was going for a final picnic over to Baker's Grove at Ostable. We went, three catboats full of us, and Van and Mabel Seabury was in the same boat. We made the grove all right, and me and Jonadab had our hands full, baking clams and chasing spiders out of the milk, and doing all the chores that makes a picnic so joyfully miserable. When the dinner dishes was washed I went off by myself to a quiet bunch of bayberry bushes half a mile from the grove and laid down to rest, being beat out.

I guess I fell asleep, and what woke me was somebody speaking close by. I was going to get up and clear out, not being in the habit of listening to other folks' affairs, but the very first words I heard showed me that 'twas best, for the feelings of all concerned, to lay still and keep on with my nap.

"Oh, no!" says Mabel Seabury, dreadful nervous and hurried-like; "oh, no! Mr. Van Wedderburn, please don't say any more. I can't listen to you, I'm so sorry."

"Do you mean that—really mean it?" asks Van, his voice rather shaky and seemingly a good deal upset. "My dear young lady, I realize that I'm twice your age and more, and I suppose that I was an old fool to hope; but I've had trouble lately, and I've been very lonely, and you have been so kind that I thought—I did hope— I— Can't you?"

"No," says she, more nervous than ever, and shaky, too, but decided. "No! Oh, no! It's all my fault. I wanted you to like me; I wanted you to like me very much. But not this way. I'm—I'm—*so* sorry. Please forgive me."

She walked on then, fast, and toward the grove, and he followed, slashing at the weeds with his cane, and acting a good deal as if he'd like to pick up his playthings and go home. When they was out of sight I set up and winked, large and comprehensive, at the scenery. It looked to me like I was going to collect Jonadab's quarter.

That night as I passed the lilac bushes by the gate, somebody steps out and grabs my arm. I jumped, looked up, and there, glaring down at me out of the clouds, was friend Jones from Providence, R. I.

"Wingate," he whispers, fierce, "who is the man? And where is he?"

"Easy," I begs. "Easy on that arm. I might want to use it again. What man?"

"That man you wrote me about. I've come down here to interview him. Confound him! Who is he?"

"Oh, it's all right now," says I. "There was an old rooster from New York who was acting too skittish to suit me, but I guess it's ll off. His being a millionaire and a stock-jobber was what scart me fust along. He's a hundred years old or so; name of Van Wedderburn."

"*What?*" he says, pinching my arm till I could all but feel his thumb and finger meet. "What? Stop joking. I'm not funny to-night."

"It's no joke," says I, trying to put my arm together again. "Van Wedderburn is his name. 'Course you've heard of him. Why! there he is now."

Sure enough, there was Van, standing like a statue of misery on the front porch of the main hotel, the light from the winder shining full on him. Jonesy stared and stared.

"Is that the man?" he says, choking up. "Was *he* sweet on Mabel?"

"Sweeter'n a molasses stopper," says I. "But he's going away in a day or so. You don't need to worry."

He commenced to laugh, and I thought he'd never stop.

"What's the joke?" I asks, after a year or so of this foolishness. "Let me in, won't you? Thought you wa'n't funny to-night."

He stopped long enough to ask one more question. "Tell me, for the Lord's sake!" says he. "Did she know who he was?"

"Sartin," says I. "So did every other woman round the place. You'd think so if——"

He walked off then, laughing himself into a fit. "Good night, old man," he says, between spasms. "See you later. No, I don't think I shall worry much."

If he hadn't been so big I cal'lated I'd have risked a kick. A man hates to be made a fool of and not know why.

A whole lot of the boarders had gone on the evening train, and at our house Van Wedderburn was the only one left. He and Mabel and me was the full crew at the breakfast-table the follering morning. The fruit season was a quiet one. I done all the talking there was; every time the broker and the housekeeper looked at each other they turned red.

Finally 'twas "chopped-hay" time, and in comes the waiter with the tray. And again we had a surprise, just like the one back in July. Percy wa'n't on hand, and Jonesy was.

But the other surprise wa'n't nothing to this one. The Seabury girl was mightily set back, but old Van was paralyzed. His eyes and mouth opened and kept on opening.

"Cereal, sir?" asks Jones, polite as ever.

"Why! why, you—you rascal!" hollers Van Wedderburn. "What are you doing here?"

"I have a few days' vacation from my position at Providence, sir," answers Jones. "I'm a waiter at present."

"Why, *Robert!*" exclaims Mabel Seabury.

Van swung around like he was on a pivot. "Do you know *him?*" he pants, wild as a coot, and pointing.

'Twas the waiter himself that answered.

"She knows me, father," he says. "In fact she is the young lady I told you about last spring; the one I intend to marry."

Did you ever see the tide go out over the flats? Well, that's the way the red slid down off old Van's bald head and across his cheeks. But it came back again like an earthquake wave. He turned to Mabel once more, and if ever there was a pleading "Don't tell" in a man's eyes, 'twas in his.

"Cereal, sir?" asks Robert Van Wedderburn, alias "Jonesy."

Well, I guess that's about all. Van Senior took it enough sight more graceful than you'd expect, under the circumstances. He went straight up to his room and never showed up till suppertime. Then he marches to where Mabel and his son was, on the porch, and says he:

"Bob," he says, "if you don't marry this young lady within a month I'll disown you, for good this time. You've got more sense than I thought. Blessed if I see who you inherit it from!" says he, kind of to himself.

Jonadab ain't paid me the quarter yet. He

says the bet was that she'd land a millionaire, and a Van Wedderburn, afore the season ended, and she did; so he figgers that he won the bet. Him and me got wedding cards a week ago, so I suppose "Jonesy" and Mabel are on their honeymoon now. I wonder if she's ever told her husband about what I heard in the bayberry bushes. Being the gamest sport, for a woman, that ever I see, I'll gamble she ain't said a word about it.